Beta

JILLIAN RINK

For Jian, Djoya, Andrea, and Kiki.
Thank you for encouraging me to finish this when it felt like it was impossible.

Playlist

Electric Touch (Taylor's Version) (From the Vault)
Taylor Swift

Let Me Down Slowly
Alec Benjamin

Something Just Like This
The Chainsmokers & Coldplay

Mastermind
Taylor Swift

Before You Read

While Beta is ultimately a happy book with a happy ending, it contains scenes and situations that may be concerning to some readers. These include moments of violence, sex work, and explicit sexual content.

One

JASPER

I sink into the moment of suspension as the symphony ends, my fellow musicians holding a collective breath. It's the best part of the opening piece of this concert: the way the final note rings through the hall, the stillness that it invokes in the listener for just a hairsbreadth before the modern world eclipses it. My hand still feels the reverberations of the string through my bow as I lift it away, letting my cello join the others even as the timpani continue vibrating from the residual perfect harmonies. The conductor smiles before offering a resounding praise.

The moment is lost, but Liz elbows me, and I know she felt it, too. If it's this good in rehearsal, it should be perfect for the performance next Saturday, a haunting warning of what the entire night's repertoire evokes.

"Mr. Jameson will be distributing the new pieces in just a moment," Giles Moran says from where he stands on the conductor's podium. His baton is stashed in his back pocket, the top button of his Oxford left undone, his thin glasses perched on the edge of his nose. He glances at the music stand in front of him and flips a page. "While he does that, let's review piece three. Violins, from the top, please."

The rest of the symphony visibly relaxes as he singles in on the tricky opening to the final piece of the performance. I make a few notes on the music before letting my cello relax against my legs and rest my bow in my lap. Mason's quick intake of breath is my only warning that Rylan's made it to our section.

"Prinicpal," he says, handing a small stack of papers to Liz on my left. "Second." His voice warms as he turns to Mason. He's been principal the last six months. We rotate twice a season in the name of equality, and he's been even more excited for the shake up than I have, saying he wants a break from the solo work to be able to focus on other individual projects in his spare time.

Rylan is unsmiling when he turns to me. "Third," he says.

His voice skates over me, sending a shiver down my spine that I mask well enough. His fingers brush mine as I take the music and hide my disappointment by the skin of my teeth. He turns to the others in our section without further comment.

Third. Damn it.

Giles finishes up with the violins as I organize the new music, ordering it by the concert schedule I keep taped to the inside cover of the small black binder I use to keep track of everything.

"Principals, if you'll make contact with me before you leave to set up sectionals. Everyone else is free to go," he says.

Mayhem breaks out moments later, the basses behind me laughing about some set of plans they have for the weekend, the low brass joining in after a few passive-aggressive comments lobbied their direction. At the first mention of football, I lose interest.

Huntley is quick to find me, wading through the rows that separate us, her oboe and English horn already packed away and slung over both shoulders. She cocks an eyebrow but doesn't say what she's clearly thinking, pursing her lips as she crosses her arms, her foot tapping to an unheard beat. She follows me to the prep space, grabbing my case so I don't have to put down my music.

We're silent as we leave the concert hall, my hands shoved into the pockets of my jeans.

"Not what you wanted, obviously," she says once we're a reasonable distance from the building.

I shake my head. "Don't get me wrong. I'm excited for Liz. It's her final season with us. She deserves to be principal again for her swan song."

Liz matched over the off season, going to one of the quarterly Matching Galas put on by the Unified Council of Alpha and Omega Designations, Inquiries, and Concerns—or Council, as most people referred to it, since the full thing was a goddamn mouthful. And definitely not the fun kind. Liz had been indecisive the last two years whether she wanted to actually be assigned to a pack. Something changed in the spring, though. One Tuesday, she walked into rehearsal and told us she would be leaving the symphony at the end of the next performance season. The next month, she was in Manhattan, dancing the night away. Everyone fawned over her pictures when she came back, appreciating all the Alpha eye candy that was there for her to enjoy.

I, however, spent too much time trying to see if Violet was in any of the photos.

Had she matched?

I was too much of a coward to look up the official public records the Council maintained. If I didn't look, I never had to face the harsh reality that she really wasn't mine. In my mind, I could still pretend we had just taken a break like a lot of young couples on the precipice of college.

Never mind that it had been nearly four years since I left

Seattle and never looked back. Or that she had dumped me before I'd ever gotten on the plane.

Huntley nods, her voice pulling me out of my thoughts. "It just sucks that it's not you. You've worked really hard for it."

"Exactly," I mutter. Though in reality, I'll get it eventually. I'm not an Omega, destined to leave permanently when the Council finally woos me into matching with a pack. And I'm not an Alpha that runs the risk of having to miss important concerts due to an Omega's heat cycle. I'm a Beta: a normal, average man with a love for music and vintage video games. Realistically, I'm one of the safest choices for principal.

Which is part of why it stings so much that I've been looked over again despite going into my third year with the L.A. Philharmonic.

"You still have that date tonight?" she asks once we're several blocks from the concert hall. I nod. "He's an Alpha, right?"

I give her my best side-eye.

She shrugs, unrepentant. "Just double checking. Remind me again why you're willing to date this Alpha but not Rylan?"

Now I scowl. "There's nothing between me and Rylan," I mutter.

Nothing but my long stares I tried to hide, my memorizing the way the two snakes intertwined on his neck, the black tattoo twisting up the side of his throat and into his hair. Nothing but my own frustration over his lack of notice, of my being so thoroughly a Beta that there was no chance in Hell I'd hold his attention long enough for him to be interested in me. On the best of days, he greeted me with a polite smile at practice. On the worst... it was like I didn't exist, his cool gaze sliding right over me.

Huntley has the audacity to *laugh in my face* before shrugging, flipping her hair over her shoulder. "And Mark doesn't resent me for having the English Horn parts."

I offer her my best glare, and she backs off, humming as we eat away the distance to our apartments. We part ways when we're a block or so away from her place.

"See you Thursday, yeah?" she asks over her shoulder. When I nod, she grins. "Excited to kick your ass at trivia again, Jas."

I shake my head and laugh. "Just watch them have a whole Zelda section this time. My time to shine!"

"That's the blond guy, right?" The joke is a staple between us, but it still has me frowning. I cock an eyebrow.

"What's that girl's name again? Rosella?" I know damn well that's not whoever she despises from Twilight.

She rolls her eyes even as she laughs. I wait until she's turned the corner before continuing on my way, adjusting my cello where it sits against my back. The next several blocks pass without me seeing them, my mind caught up with thoughts of Violet—and Rylan, since I've decided to be a complete and utter masochist today. What is it about me that just fixates on the people I *know* I can never have?

I shake my head, unlocking the door to my ground floor apartment that has certainly seen better days, pushing it open while pulling my phone from my pocket and opening a missed text from my brother. The distinct sound of water splashing steals my attention, and I glance up from the inappropriate meme Luke sent me.

You have *got* to be joking.

Two

JASPER

I close the door, rushing to the kitchen and setting my messenger bag on the small sliver of counter before perching my cello on the too-small table. It takes me a minute to figure out which maintenance line is for emergencies, but the lady on the other end is nice enough about getting someone sent to me. She gives me an estimated wait time before hanging up. I shove the phone back into my pocket. I blow out a breath and look around my studio apartment.

The apartment that is now under four inches of standing water.

Muttering a string of curses that would have my mother red-faced, I cross the space, toeing the basket full of clothes in front of the TV stand I had planned to deal with after rehearsal today.

Correction: I toe the basket full of *soaking wet* clothes that are now too water-logged to do anything with until I can take them down to the building's laundry room and dry them again.

I glare at the offending water pipe that's broken in the ceiling, gushing enough water that the drywall has crumbled and fallen in large chunks to the floor. Before I can decide what to attempt to salvage first, there's two quick, hard knocks on the door.

"Maintenance." The voice is muffled, but the irritation is clear enough.

I cross the small space, opening the door before the person can knock again. The maintenance guy stands on my threshold, hands tucked into the pockets of his worn jeans, a scowl making his harsh cheekbones so sharp they could cut glass.

"The note says there's water—"

He cuts off with a rough curse as I open the door wide enough for him to see around me. Without another comment, he pulls his phone from his back pocket and dials someone, taking a single step into the apartment, grimacing as the water splashes over his tennis shoes.

"Yeah, it's Nick. Unit 105 is flooded," he says. There's indistinct muttering from the other end of the call. "About four inches. Burst pipe in the shared wall."

He hangs up a minute later without further comment and crosses the apartment to the locked utility closet tucked into the far corner. He raises an eyebrow as he moves my desk out of the way, unlocking the door and reaching in before I can manage to ask him anything.

"You got the mandatory renters insurance?" The man doesn't look up from where he's messing with something in the utility closet. The water slows to a dribble nearly immediately, the drips coming slower until they stop entirely.

When I offer a yes, he nods.

"I'd get them on the phone. You're not going to be here for a while."

With a resigned sigh, I open the closet door and pull down my suitcase, throwing in all the still untouched clothing stored under my bed, miraculously dry despite sitting in drawers touching the floor. Points to Ikea, I guess. The maintenance guy leaves while I'm collecting everything from the bathroom, muttering something about a shop-vac.

I send a text to Huntley while he's gone. She calls me before I even manage to set the suitcase on the now-crowded two person table.

"Are you serious?" she asks the moment I pick up. When I offer a terse affirmative, she curses. "I'll call around and see if anyone has a spare room right now. And you can crash at my place for tonight if you want."

I run my hand through my hair, tipping my head back and looking at the ceiling, not seeing the small patterns in the textured drywall as I let my eyes relax and blur out.

"That'd be great," I say.

"Give me ten minutes, and I'll be there."

She hangs up without any niceties, but that's Huntley. And me. There's just certain dynamics that happen when you've been friends for multiple years.

A notification flashes across the top of my phone, and I curse again.

> Sorry, apartment problems. You down for postponing?

> Totally fine. You good?

I smirk, ignoring the butterflies in my stomach. We've been chatting for the last couple weeks after matching on a local queer dating app. It took all my courage to finally ask him out on Saturday, and I hate that I'm having to readjust the date already.

> Should be fine, just needing to sort through insurance.

I tuck my phone away once he confirms we're good to go for a couple nights from now. Putting my head down, I focus on getting together everything that can be salvaged, packing what I can into the suitcase and then moving on to the empty laundry basket tucked in the small closet. By some small cosmic fortune, the fridge is nearly empty, so there isn't anything really to pack away for food, so I'm able to focus on my concert attire and electronics.

I'm just finishing packing out the TV stand when the maintenance guy returns, an impressively large shop-vac in tow. Just behind him is Huntley, her backpack slung over one shoulder, another hard-sided suitcase rolling beside her. She cocks an eyebrow but doesn't say anything, picking up the suitcase and trading it for my packed one, opening it on the small table before I can even give a greeting.

"Thanks," I mutter, filling the new bag with the rest of my nightstand and desk, doing my best to not scratch anything overly important without moving too slowly.

"Should have an update for you by the end of the week," the man says, running an extension cord from the hallway rather than risking any of the outlets in the apartment. When I nod, he continues, "This is the worst I've seen, but Jack says it'll be a few weeks. I'd plan for four and hope for three."

"Sounds good," I say. "Thank you."

He nods and then flips on the vacuum, effectively drowning out any more conversation. Huntley grabs the suitcase and stages it beside my own while I stack the laundry basket of electronics on top of the wet clothes and then sling my cello over my shoulders again. The ten blocks to her place are going to be grueling, but I'm not about to complain about it.

"Want to dry those a bit first?" she asks once I've closed the door, cutting the sound of the vacuum in half. With a nod, I head deeper into the building instead of toward the street.

Huntley's phone goes off while I'm loading the clothes into one of the dryers, and she steps back into the hallway to answer it. I use the time to sort through my own phone, ignoring my brother again and confirming the new time for the date.

I'm folding the damp clothes when she comes back into the room. I cock an eyebrow when she bites her lip and messes with the belt loops of her jeans.

"What's wrong?" I ask.

She shakes her head. "Someone has an open room for as long as you need it."

Relief rushes through me.

"You're not going to like it, though," she says before I can say anything. I finish the folding and then readjust the baskets, prepping to carry everything to her place.

"I'll take anything, Huntley. A member of the band is better than figuring out double rent for the next several weeks."

Huntley laughs, though it feels desperate rather than exuberant.

"You might change your mind." I shrug. She doesn't hesitate, her voice dropping between us like a bomb. "It's Rylan."

"*Fuck*."

Three

RYLAN

I toss the phone onto the couch, biting out a low curse before running my hands over my face. Jasper fucking Miller is going to stay here for *weeks*. As if seeing him nearly every day at rehearsal isn't torture enough.

Why the hell did I say yes?

I blow out a breath and walk into the extra bedroom, going through the motions of making sure it's picked up enough for someone to stay here. I pull both of my guitars off the wall, digging the stands out of the closet.

Of course, I know why I said yes. It's unspoken code that you help out another member of the orchestra when they need something. They'd all do it for me. Some of them *have* done it for me. But, fuck, I don't want it to be *Jasper* that needs help right now.

I can barely keep my eyes off of him as it is. Having him in my space? It's going to be nearly impossible to keep up my feigned indifference, my ruse of complete disinterest in him. And that's going to be a problem. I'd flirted with him relentlessly the first few months he joined the philharmonic three years ago. He was cordial, even friendly, but at no point did he reciprocate.

So why can I not manage to get him out of my head, even now?

The two soft knocks on my door mean I'm out of time to muse—or spiral, as some would probably call it. I set down the last of the guitars in the living room and then open the front door, holding my breath the entire time. Huntley greets me with a too-aware smile, her hazel eyes sparkling. I scowl, and her smile widens. Before I can say anything, she's stepping into the living room, leaving the person of my greatest sexual torment standing on the threshold, two laundry baskets in his hands.

I smooth out my expression and force my body to be unresponsive, offering him a polite nod as he steps into the apartment.

"Thanks," he says.

"Sure thing," I mutter. Pointing toward the extra bedroom, I say, "Feel free to take up whatever space you need in there. Should all be empty."

Huntley takes both baskets from him, heading into the bedroom.

Like the fucking meddling traitor she is. I make a note to pester her about it tomorrow at rehearsal. Jasper blows out a breath, messing with the chain of a thin silver necklace tucked under his crew neck. I don't dare move from my spot beside the door, shoving my hands into my pockets to keep from doing something absolutely asinine.

"The maintenance guy said it would be a few weeks. Insurance is convinced it'll take three," Jasper says after a moment. "I'll do what I can to get out of your hair as quickly as possible. I know having a roommate isn't what you signed up for."

I shrug and run a hand through my hair, scratching at my tattoo. "It is what it is," I say eventually. "Don't stress too much about it."

He offers a single nod and then grabs the suitcases Huntley abandoned, rolling them into the spare bedroom. Against my better judgment—who knew I even had a good one, yeah?—I follow a few steps behind him and lean against the threshold, crossing my arms, trying to exude calm, collected control. Huntley and Jasper make a good team, working together seamlessly. They don't bump into each other, don't accidentally go to the same space at the same moment. It's mesmerizing.

At least that's what I'm going to tell myself is mesmerizing.

Because it's definitely not Jasper's ass in those jeans. And certainly not the way it fills out those jeans as he leans down and grabs something he dropped on the ground.

Blood rushes to my groin, and I sigh, adjusting my stance, ignoring the sudden bergamot bleeding from me as I scent for a goddamn Beta.

"Need anything?" I ask.

Huntley glances up with a smirk across those lips, and I scowl at her. She cocks an eyebrow but doesn't say anything, glancing over at Jasper where he's paused in front of the night stand.

Staring at me.

His gaze flicks down, noting my erection pushing against my sweats, before darting back to Huntley. It's easy enough to see the conclusion he's drawn.

"We're fine," he says, polite as ever despite it being a clear dismissal. He turns back for the nightstand, adjusting something in the top drawer.

I scowl at Huntley again as she bites her lip before closing the door.

This is going to be a long three fucking weeks.

"Of course, he's a fucking morning person." The comment is useless, but it makes me feel better as I cross from my ensuite to the closet, grabbing a set of briefs and pulling them on before picking out a set of jeans for the day. "Everyone has to have a downside. Lucky for me, he has two: he likes mornings, and he thinks I'm straight."

I shake my head, blowing out a breath and running my hands through my hair, making it even messier.

Just walk out there, Rylan. He's your goddamn roommate, not the fucking police.

Maybe this time I'll actually listen to myself. I look around my bedroom, trying to come up with another thing to do to justify hiding in here. But the shelves are spotless and the clothes are actually put away. Even my music is organized within an inch of its life.

Fuck it.

I cross the room and pull the door open, too aggressively, and walk into the living room before I can decide to take a second shower. Jasper is quietly making something at the stove, his back to me. I breathe out a sigh—of relief. Definitely relief. There's no way I'm disappointed he didn't catch me all hung up over him out here.

He glances over his shoulder as I grab one of the protein shakes from the fridge, shaking it before opening it and drinking it all in three large gulps. I pretend I don't see the way his throat ripples with his swallow.

"Morning," he says. "I'd say 'good' but then I'd still be asleep and not waiting for this stove to work so I can get to my private lessons before rehearsal."

I frown. "What's wrong with the stove?"

He shrugs, stepping to the side. "The Jasper Touch,

apparently. Mom's given me shit for it since I was a teen. I'm just lucky it's only snapped bows and not the cello."

I cock an eyebrow as I toss the empty shake into the recycle and then cross the kitchen. Bows still cost hundreds of dollars.

"How many have you snapped?"

Jasper frowns. A rock settles in my gut, but I ignore it. Just a lovely side effect of being Alpha: I don't like hurting those that are dependent on me. I viciously tell those instincts that Jasper *isn't*, in fact, one of those people, but they just ignore me.

I finally register the blue sauté pan Jasper holds.

"Oh. It's the wrong pan," I say, grabbing the other from the rack above the stove. "Induction cooktops have certain types of pans that work. I haven't gone through all my extras yet."

Jasper nods, taking the frying pan from me and switching them out, transferring the uncooked French toast without managing to drop a single piece of egg onto the ground.

"Thanks."

I back up several steps, trying to ignore the way my body responds to his nearness. The distance, of course, brings the rest of him into sharper focus. Just when I've managed to keep my dick from getting involved in all this, I notice what he's wearing.

Jasper in a tux is devastating. In gray sweats? He's every wet dream I've ever had come to life.

They hug his ass and ride low on his hips, and the simple tee he's wearing rides up every time he does something to the French toast, revealing that sliver of skin just above the waistband. He twists, and I can see the hard line of his hip.

I force a swallow and take another step back, trying to remember that we're fucking coworkers. Sure, people fuck around between sections all the time. But Jasper is practically orchestra royalty. Everyone adores him. If I fuck him and he hates it, it'll ruin my already precarious standing with the concertmaster.

"You want a ride to rehearsal?" I ask.

Jasper glances up before shaking his head. "I have a date afterwards, so I'll just take a ride share."

A date.

Right.

I ignore the roaring in my ears, the flash of anger that heats my skin, the clench in my belly. I shove all the pieces of my Alpha instincts rumbling uneasily just below the surface until I can't feel them, sense them, until I no longer have the urge to *rut*. I might need to swing by the Council's heat facility and see if there's a fucking Omega that needs someone. Because there's no way I will survive three weeks of my instincts doing this.

I force my voice to be calm. "Sounds like a plan."

I turn and head back to my room, managing to grab one of my electric guitars from the stand in the living room—and pretend I don't notice how my hands shake.

Four

DOMINIC

By the time I make it to the end of the arcade bar's block, I'm ready to punch someone just to feel their nose break. My phone vibrates again in my pocket, and I snarl, switching it off without looking at it. As if my father didn't make it perfectly clear in his office two hours ago what is expected of me before I turn thirty.

Form a pack. Get matched. Have children. Just like my brothers. Unlike my brothers, though, he's held my goddamn trust fund over my head. Not that I overly need it at the moment. But if I want out of the family business? That trust fund is my golden ticket.

I run my hands over my head and through my hair, pulling on the ends just enough that it hurts. The pain helps clear my head.

The first one—forming a pack—isn't the worst expectation. It's all but assumed that I'll find a group of people and register with the Council just like any other Alpha in my family's business. Getting matched isn't nearly as appealing. Allowing someone else to decide my sexual and romantic partner? No, thank you. And having children? Absolutely not. I'd get a vasectomy yesterday if my designation didn't make it impossible.

"*Accidenti*," I mutter, shoving my hands in my pockets and heading up the street.

I try to put the whole mess out of my mind, focusing instead on the profile picture of the man I'm meeting tonight: blond hair, blue eyes, a smile that probably gets him laid without trying. The definition of carefree surfer man, really, though there was no indication in any of our conversations that he actually surfs. He's a musician, which is something I can appreciate. Any artist managing to survive in this city without generational wealth to keep them afloat has my respect.

There's a decent crowd milling around despite it being the middle of the week. I take a deep breath to steady myself, noting both bouncers standing near the doors as well as the security guard situated near the bar at the back of the building, visible from where I walk outside. A small group of men chat just outside the door, cigarettes lit and dangling from their loose holds. My fingers twitch, but I ignore the sudden urge to ask them for one. A blond man in a dark gray polo and jeans looks up as I cross the street in front of the arcade bar we'd agreed on last week, and I'm met with those same blue eyes. Somehow, they manage to be even more striking in person. He tucks his phone into his pocket and heads toward me, keeping his hands loose at his sides, a half-smile tilting his lips.

"Dominic?" he asks.

He stands the same height as me, his build lithe but sturdy, the cotton of his shirt stretching taut across his chest and biceps. His voice is smooth as silk, a lightness to it that has me thinking most people find him comfortable to be around. *Charismatic* in its purest form, that's what Jasper is. And he is positive he's a

Beta? I focus on his breathing, his small movements, waiting to see if any of my instincts roar to the forefront, but they remain strangely—blissfully—quiet. Definitely not an Omega, then. I offer my hand, and he takes it easily enough, the callouses from his playing catching on my own—though mine developed from less-than-upright means.

"Nice to finally see you," he continues, running a hand through his hair and loosing a pent-up breath. "Sorry for having to reschedule."

I wave off the apology and urge him inside with a subtle touch on his waist. He leans into the brush of my fingers, and my breath hitches for a heartbeat.

"How is everything with the apartment, then?" I ask to distract myself.

It's poor form to take a date straight back to my place—or even my car—so early on. But the subtle cedar scent of his cologne has me thinking of reenacting the occasional hookups I've had with women: lock the bathroom and see how many people are pissed when we walk out twenty minutes later disheveled to all hell.

He shrugs, the light dimming in his eyes for a moment.

"It's managed," he says.

The need to fix the problem so that his eyes don't dim again roars through me, but I tamp it back as we cross the threshold.

The bar is bustling, the lights of the pinball machines flashing in the low lighting, the colors distorted from the orange glow of the sunset. The security guard near the bar adjusts his stance, his hands dropping from his pockets, his eyes growing keen as Jasper and I take up seats beside each other at the bar top. The music isn't overbearing, and the chatter is a manageable volume so far, so the bartender leaning *that far* into Jasper's space instantly sets me off.

I lean into him, too, trailing my hand down his leg, and smirk when he presses into my touch.

"Double whiskey on the rocks," Jasper says in response to what the blonde woman asked. It shames me that I was too focused on making sure he liked me more that I didn't hear the question. She glances at me, her eyes catching on where my hand is clearly not on my own body under the table, then purses her lips.

"You?" she asks.

"Whiskey and amaretto, please," I say, keeping polite despite her disinterest in me as a whole. No one needs me to lose my cool over some bartender that doesn't even know who my family is, especially when getting out of my family's business is my top priority. If I'm successful, then it won't matter when someone doesn't recognize me. Not to mention, I won't have a literal get-out-of-jail-free card anymore.

She deposits both drinks in front of us and offers a sultry smile to Jasper. He gives a warm thanks before twisting toward me, his knee brushing my own. That seems to get it through to her that we're not just friends meeting up for a late night drink in the middle of the work week. Her shoulders drop as she walks away, but I focus on Jasper instead of marking her movements anymore. His lips shape around the rim of the glass, his throat moving with the small sip he takes of the alcohol.

I don't try to play down my scent as it permeates the air around us both. The security guard raises an eyebrow, but Jasper doesn't seem to notice at all.

Cazzo. Definitely a Beta.

A less confident man—Alpha—might take his lack of response as disinterest. The fluttering of his heartbeat in his throat assures me that it isn't.

"How long have you been playing with the philharmonic?" I ask after a few minutes.

Jasper's lips quirk for a moment as he sets his whiskey down.

"This is my third season," he says, tracing the rim of the tumbler. "Though I'm curious how you know that's where I play. I intentionally don't list it in my profile information."

I smirk and take a sip of my own drink.

"It's a side effect of working in my family's business." My voice is dry, sarcastic even.

Jasper grunts but doesn't push for more information. He shifts in his seat, leaning closer toward me. Those instincts I detest settle under his subtle movements and his desire for more contact. I shouldn't be as pleased about that as I am, but I burned "shouldn't" the first time I saw the life drain from a man's eyes.

"Do you enjoy it?" Jaspers asks, taking another sip of his whiskey. "Your family's business?"

The scowl is fast and fierce, and I do nothing to hide it. He lifts an eyebrow but doesn't shy away, so I run my finger along the inside of his knee and luxuriate in the rippling of his throat as he swallows and licks his lips.

"No," I offer. "It's something I've wanted out of since I understood what it was and what would be expected of me."

Jasper's gaze brightens with understanding, and he nods. "I can relate to that."

The roar of a group of guys celebrating setting a record on one of the pinball machines steals my attention. They clap and cheer and high five each other, and Jasper laughs.

"Do you enjoy playing?" I ask, watching as he takes in the group again.

He offers a shy smile, his cheeks turning rosy. "My friend and I have a monthly date here. Loser pays the drink tab."

My curiosity piques. Which friend? Are they *just* friends or something more? Jealousy roars through me, but I force it to heel.

"Which one is your favorite to play?"

His gaze flicks to the back corner, the machines along the back wall mostly shadowed, their neon lights the only illumination.

"The one on the far wall, all the way to the right."

Tucked behind the wall, then, where I can't currently see.

It's like this man *wants* me to find a dark corner and fuck him until he can't breathe, can't walk straight. My body finally overrides my urging, my dick hardening and pressing against the zipper of my slacks. The need to mark him roars up in me, stealing my breath for a heartbeat. I take a sip of the drink still in my hand, using the burn of the alcohol to calm my instincts.

"Want to see who wins?" I ask, squeezing his knee and taking another large sip of the drink.

His eyes light up, and I bask in the simple happiness that making him excited creates in me.

It's moments like this that make me so resistant to my father's wishes. How could the Council—full of pretentious, out-of-touch snobs—possibly create by force something as fulfilling as natural attraction?

He starts to grab for his back pocket, presumably to pay for his drink, but I'm quick to shake my head. He relents immediately, sitting back. His eyes are keen, bright, as I pull a larger bill than needed and set it on the bar top. I scoop up my drink and offer my hand to Jasper, forcing the purr to silence at his immediate touch.

"What does the winner get?" he asks, his smile wide. He maneuvers around the growing crowd with ease. I sip the alcohol, marking each small movement he makes—as well as the security guard that subtly follows us across the bar.

"How about a kiss?"

Five

JASPER

The soft smirk that graces Dominic's lips makes me agree in a heartbeat. It doesn't help that his golden skin and brown eyes combine with high cheekbones, making him the literal definition of a wet dream.

"Anywhere they want," I say.

My voice is breathy, but I don't apologize for it.

That smirk grows to a full smile, and my stomach heats, a thread of it drifting lower.

"Go ahead," he says, holding out his hand—fingers still wrapped around the small tumbler—toward the machine. He tucks his other into his slacks, his watch perfectly placed so it's just visible over the hem of the fabric.

Everything about Dominic screams old money. His clothes are clearly a designer label, perfectly tailored to his body but not over-the-top. The thin necklace he keeps tucked under the collar of his polo is probably worth more than I make in a month. That watch certainly is. His brown eyes are cunning just as much as they are deep. It makes me want to see what they look like heated, when he's at the edge of his control, trying to hold back from rutting.

Not that he would do that to me. A sharp pang fills my chest and snaps me out of the moment. I finish the whiskey and set the empty glass on the small table wedged between the pinball table and the wall, careful to not touch the other cups already left behind by others.

My favorite table is tucked into the corner because it's the least flashy of the twenty or so scattered through the bar. It's themed after a pier, the colors muted instead of neon, the jackpots simple and straightforward. No flashy side games, no frustrating inner mechanics that are as much luck as they are skill. This table? It just sees you as you are and demands that to be enough.

There's probably a parallel there somewhere, but I refuse to look too closely at it, especially tonight. Dominic takes a step, settling in behind me, looking at the table over my shoulder. The first two balls are worthless, my attention on the enigmatic man behind me rather than the table. On the final ball, by some miracle, I manage to focus on the game, unlocking the easiest of the jackpots available before missing one of the sharp rebounds and draining the ball. The table switches to second player, and Dominic hums, a low, sensual noise in the back of his throat that has me trying to remember how to breathe.

"Simple enough," he murmurs just behind my ear, reaching around me to set the alcohol next to my empty glass. Goosebumps race down my neck, and I shudder in a breath. "Let's see how I manage, then."

I step to the side so he can take his turn, keeping a half-step to the left. For the first time I can remember, my eyes are locked on the player rather than the table while he plays. His forearms flex with each flip of the bumpers, his hair falls forward onto his forehead each time he leans over the table to see the upper portion better. Hell, even his throat ripples and moves as he clenches his jaw each time he gutters the ball. My body responds to all the details, my dick taking interest, and I adjust my weight, trying to take the pressure off without being conspicuous. By the time he drains the final ball with a sharp, quiet curse in what I'm nearly confident is Italian, my skin burns with how turned on I am, and the room has dimmed to a distant background.

"I am not used to losing," he murmurs as he turns toward me.

I offer my easiest smile, trying to keep the depth of my interest in him hidden for a while longer. Plenty of people over the years have flirted with me but never once attempted to go on from there, have never asked me on a date or responded when I've asked for a second. There's no guarantee he finds me the same level of interesting.

Or even more than that: he might want to designate as a pack.

"It's very Beta of you," I say, trying to ease into the question. He tilts his head. "We tend to be less concerned with winning and losing compared to Alphas."

"True," he murmurs.

He takes a step into me, and the incessant noise fades away in my mind, joining the din of the bar around us. The question fades with them. His brown eyes are flecked with gold, the lights of the pinball tables highlighting his sharp, high cheekbones and narrow jaw.

"One request, Jasper," he murmurs. I cock an eyebrow in silent question. "You do not share this kiss with the rest of the world."

Another piece of him clicks into place, right next to why he would have calluses from his family's business while dressing like a businessman and his ability to figure out everything about me before ever meeting me in person.

Mafia.

The word flashes through me, nearly as fast and as hot as the desire a few moments before.

Of course I would manage to have a member of the mafia interested in me. Another moment of the Jasper Touch at work, breaking everything that I come into contact with. I force a deep breath, trying to figure out if the risk is worth it. Is this something he would even be willing to display openly at some point? Or will I always be the secret option in the corner while he goes off to be matched with an Omega?

I tip my head toward the front of the bar and shove my hands into my pockets, trying to keep my indecision off my face.

"Let's take a walk then," I offer, keeping my voice light, if a little breathless.

He purses his lips, gaze scanning me before nodding. His hand settles on my low back, and I can't resist leaning into the touch. If one night is all I'm going to get with this man, then I might as well enjoy the pieces he lets me experience.

"Where did you park?" he asks once we're outside, stepping off to the side to avoid another group trying to get into the bar.

"I took a ride share," I say.

He nods and guides me to a parking lot at the end of the block, his steps sure, his shoulders relaxed. The walk helps clear my head, all those insidious thoughts quieting. Even if he never calls me back, I want to have fun in the moment.

The lot is nearly full despite it being a Wednesday night, and it takes a couple minutes to navigate the space to where he's parked. A small, red Maserati sits amidst the more standard cars. Sport cars aren't really my thing, but even I can appreciate the luxury of the vehicle.

Mafia. The word reverberates through me again.

Dominic turns to me and leans against the car, a small smile curving his lips.

"I still owe you a kiss," he murmurs, his hands sliding into his pockets.

Fire licks through my veins, and I step into him until our chests brush and our mouths are a hairsbreadth apart.

"What if this isn't the type of kiss I wanted?" I ask, letting my voice lower and my eyes flick to his mouth for a moment. I want to see his eyes darken again, want to see him lean over me in a sign of possession even if he didn't realize he was doing it. "What if I wanted something... messier?"

He stills, his hands landing on my hips, his grip so light it's practically nonexistent.

"I'd apologize for bringing this particular car," he murmurs, his words gaining a heavier accent. "And then promise to make it work anyway."

I hum, closing the last bit of space between us, letting our bodies touch from chest to hip. He growls low in his throat even as he cocks an eyebrow. I mess with the belt loops of his slacks, twisting them around my fingers as I try to decide what direction I want to take this.

When I don't say anything, he whispers, "Perhaps I could give you a rain check for the kiss. You could redeem it later when it better suits your tastes."

Damn, that's the craftiest invitation to set up a second date that I've ever experienced. I grin.

"I accept," I say.

And then I'm kissing him, soft and slow, trying to memorize the feel of his lips and the taste of his skin. He lets me lead for just long enough that I lean into him and let my thoughts fade away. The moment I melt against him, his hands dig into my hips, and he's twisting us around, pressing me into the sports car and forcing my legs wide enough for him to stand between. His erection digs into my hip, and I groan. Before I can let my hands wander any lower than his chest, he pulls away, his breathing ragged, the smell of citrus overwhelming the space around us.

I made an Alpha scent.

The realization is startling enough that I don't realize he's pulling away until it's too late to kiss him again.

"Let me take you home, Jasper," he murmurs.

Six

JASPER

"How can he afford to keep the A/C so low?"

It's positively freezing as I force myself out of bed. I stretch my neck and ignore the aching sting of the hickeys left behind by Dominic. We didn't recreate my original kissing idea, but we sure got damn close.

A shiver wracks my body, and I mutter a low curse.

"If I wanted to experience winter, I would have moved to fucking Michigan," I say under my breath, crossing the room to the small dresser I've taken over as my own since being here the last few days.

Dropping to a crouch, I dig through the bottom drawer and try to find one of the hoodies I still have despite LA never really being cold enough to justify using them. A dark red catches my eye, and I breathe a sigh, letting the tension bleed from my shoulders.

Is it completely messed up that I'm wearing a hoodie Violet

gave me years ago when I'm covered in hickeys from another lover?

Absolutely.

I run my hands through my hair before stretching my arms above my head, reveling in the burn of my shoulders, and ignore the stab of guilt that still hits every time I think about moving on from her.

It's been four *fucking* years, for crying out loud.

She's probably already matched and settled down with a pack at this point.

Shaking my head to force the thoughts away, I go through the motions of getting ready for the day, preparing myself for the marathon that Thursdays always are due to the double rehearsals. Once the room is cleaned and my clothes are tucked away in preparation for my next trip to the laundry room, I check the time on my phone.

"Ah, shit." I curse and hurry into the main room to put together a quick breakfast. Rehearsal's in less than an hour, and the public transport in this section of town is less than ideal. Rylan glances up from where he's going through paperwork at the island counter.

"Seattle? Really?" he asks, his voice still raspy with sleep. It goes straight to my dick, but I do my best to ignore it.

"Lived there my whole life. Seemed natural to do undergrad there, too," I say. I leave out the fact that I stayed in Seattle—and turned down the full ride another school had offered me my sophomore year in college—to be nearer to Violet while she finished out high school.

Fuck all that it ended up mattering.

I force my thoughts away from that whole last week I lived there and focus instead on grabbing the leftover sandwich from yesterday's lunch. As I grab the binder of music from where I'd left it perched on the small side table beside the lounge chair, my curiosity gets the best of me.

"Is that something for the orchestra?" I ask before taking a bite.

Rylan shakes his head before carefully flipping over one of the sheets, covering any pertinent info.

"It's my registration renewal with the Council," he says after a moment. He scratches at the twin snakes that run up the right side of his neck.

Unease has my stomach knotting up. "I didn't realize you were registered with a pack." I keep the comment neutral, doing my best to keep the stab of jealousy out of my voice. "Have you been to any of the galas?"

Have you seen Violet?

Rylan scoffs. "I wish."

That stab deepens to a sharp twist, but I force myself to breathe through it.

"This is my registration for the Haven. I have to supply updated information every three months." He continues on, completely at ease. He pulls a pen from his pocket and signs the bottom of one of the pages before reorganizing the papers and slipping them into a small backpack tucked next to the door. "If the right group were to want to register, I would. But for now, I use the heat facility as a way to keep everything from becoming too overbearing."

"Oh."

That sounds pathetic. *Oh.* It even came out breathy.

Rylan glances over his shoulder. I force another bite of the sandwich, though it tastes like sandpaper now. His gaze grows sharp.

"We should get going," he says after a minute. "You can ride with me so you don't have to figure out which bus will get you there on time."

I don't have the heart to turn him down. I should, I know. Nothing good will come from me being in an even smaller space with him. I'm barely holding it together as it is.

"Let me grab my cello," I say instead.

Always choosing the masochistic option, that's me.

Four hours of grueling run-throughs in preparation for Saturday do nothing to tamper the restless, frustrated energy leftover from the car ride with Rylan. My fingers burn and my arms ache, but I'm still consumed with the desire to shove Rylan against a wall just to force him to react to me, to show me if he has any interest at all. That look he gave me just before we left? I can't forget it. It's like it's become tattooed to the backs of my eyes. Every time I close them to focus on the music, he's there with that sharp gaze seeing more than I wanted him to.

"We're going out after the concert, right?" Liz asks Mason and me as we gather our music.

"Of course," he replies. He looks over my shoulder and waves, a smile lighting his face. "Huntley! You said there was a bar you wanted to try, right?"

Huntley grabs my music and says, "Yeah, it's in the Arts District and gets a ton of good reviews. Thought we could check it out."

Liz laughs. "Translation: Huntley has a potential date and wants to scope out the location ahead of time."

Huntley shrugs and flips her hair, following us as we head to the staging room to get our cellos put away. "You guys all right with that?"

"We get to know everything about this date," Mason says. Huntley grins and pulls out her phone. I move past them, working on getting everything situated while my friends rave over whoever has caught Huntley's attention this week.

"Jas!" Liz calls for me. All three of them are looking at me, Huntley's phone in Mason's outstretched hand, a picture of a beautiful brunette woman mid-laugh taking up most of the screen. "What do you think?"

"She's beautiful," I say, snapping the cello case closed and standing it up on its side. Huntley hands me my music, and I pull the backpack out of my storage locker and tuck it into the largest pocket. They go back to discussing the upcoming date, diving into outfit choices and best hairstyles for the vibe. I tune them out, grabbing my phone from the small side pocket of my backpack.

A single text message greets me, and the lingering frustration over Rylan dissipates at last.

Sunday night open?

My body heats, and I can't help but laugh under my breath, giddiness overtaking my unease over whatever is happening with Rylan.

"I haven't seen you look like that all year, Jas," Huntley says. She crosses her arms as I glance up at her, but her smile doesn't falter. Mason and Liz look up from the dating profile, curiosity painted across their faces. I roll my eyes and send a quick text back to Dominic.

Absolutely. Your turn to pick the venue?

I'll grab you at 6.

"Who's the lucky person?" Liz asks the moment I've tucked my phone into my back pocket. When my cheeks heat, she smirks and hands her borrowed phone back to Huntley. "Tell me you have a picture, too! I want to fawn over all of them."

Mason shakes his head and deals with his cello. "As if you don't have *multiple options* to fawn over every single day, Liz. Don't think we've forgotten you have four Alphas wrapped around your finger."

Liz sticks out her tongue and crosses her arms. "It's not the same, Mason!"

A couple of the other musicians pause getting ready to leave, but no one says anything. Liz is prone to these little moments. It's something most of us are going to miss when she retires after this season.

"Besides, Zach has been gone all week on a training mission." Liz's tone takes on a worried feel, and she crosses her arms over her stomach, her eyes widening. Mason touches her arm in silent acknowledgement, and the rare moment of her being a vulnerable Omega dissipates as quickly as it came.

Huntley doesn't give up on her quest for information.

"Is it that guy you saw yesterday?"

I don't answer, but that's answer enough for her.

"Oh shit!" she grins and elbows me again. "He must have really liked you! Tell me you're going out again."

I shoulder my cello and cross the room, and she keeps stride without issue. The others follow close behind.

"Come on, tell us, Jas!" Liz pokes my side. "What's his name? How many times have you gone out? Have you gone exclusive?"

Rylan walks through the door as we're just getting to it. He offers a quick apology but doesn't look at me as he steps to the side, giving us enough room to get through.

"I think I have a photo, actually," Huntley says. "He sent me one when they started chatting on the dating app."

I could kill her and only feel a small bit of remorse.

Rylan pauses just beyond the door, his hand tightening on

the door frame. Something too similar to guilt twists my gut, though I refuse to figure out why.

The words come pouring out of my mouth before I even realize what I'm saying.

"Let it rest," I say. "It was just one date. No big deal. If something else happens, I'll tell you." All three of them purse their lips, and Huntley keeps navigating something on her phone. Time for more drastic measures. "Huntley, what's her name? When are you meeting up?"

Huntley gives me a long, unimpressed look, knowing exactly what I'm doing.

"Liz," a male voice says beyond us.

Liz legitimately *squeaks* and then takes off, leaving her cello behind as she catapults herself into a tall man's arms, not bothering to double check that he'll actually catch her. He buries his nose into her throat, breathing deeply even as she gushes and laughs and twists her hands into his hair. Neither seem to mind that he's still in military fatigues, though the man standing beside them sighs.

"I missed you," she says eventually.

"You owe me fifty, Zach," says the other man as he steps around them and grabs the cello. He gives each of us a nod and then leads Liz and her Alpha out of the space, both of them completely lost in each other.

My chest tightens, but I force myself to ignore it. What wouldn't I give to have that moment with someone? For some reason, I glance back at Rylan. He's staring at me, that same look sharpening his eyes that he had earlier in the apartment. Heat flashes through me.

"Suppose that means she's not coming to trivia," Mason says.

Huntley laughs, breaking my attention. "She's too busy coming another way."

I roll my eyes and glance back toward Rylan just in time to

see him duck into the staging room, the dual snakes of his tattoo flashing under the lights. That same foreign sensation twists in my gut. Huntley elbows me when she realizes I'm not paying attention.

"You still good for trivia tonight?"

I force a swallow to wet my suddenly dry mouth. "Yeah, H. Of course I am."

Seven

DOMINIC

"**C**ome now, son," my father says, leaning back into his chair, "you are not truly serious about wanting out of this."

Keeping a scowl off my face is damn near impossible.

Accidenti.

How many times am I going to have to have this conversation with him for it to become clear that I do, in fact, want out of being the son of a Made Man? My brothers love it. Victor can't wait to take over the business from our father despite his not Matching yet. Lorenzo loves being involved in everything: the fights, the bets, the girls. I'm the odd one out, the one that can't stand it, the one that vomited everywhere the first time I had to kill a man myself.

Forcing the thoughts away, I nod my head once, slowly.

"Yes, father, I am," I say after another minute.

His frown settles in, the lines of his face deepening.

Looking at him is like looking in a time machine set to thirty years in the future. While my brothers take after our mother, I'm my father through and through. The dark hair, the brown eyes, the sharp cheekbones and narrow chin. There's none of the softness my mother has. Certainly not her vibrant green eyes that remind me of the palm trees near the ocean.

He blows out a breath before leaning forward.

"Very well, *Domenico*," he murmurs. He pulls a nondescript manila envelope from a drawer and sets it on the desk between us. "I will not expect anything else from you regarding the business under one condition."

Only one? That's lowered from the three requirements he was adamant about the last time I brought it up several days ago.

"What is it?" I ask.

He purses his lips.

"You are to register with the Council and submit to being matched."

The disgust settles in my gut faster than I can take in a breath.

No.

I breathe through the visceral reaction, keeping those instincts locked down tight before they can cause problems for me. For all his ruthlessness, my father is still a Beta. He doesn't understand the bone-deep craving that drives me to restlessness when I ignore it for too long or the swift violence that rises when something—or someone—in my keeping is threatened.

"It can take years for a pack to Match." My voice is calm, collected, but my father still grunts, his disapproval clear in the set of his shoulders and tapping of his fingers on the envelope. "Am I to wait years to be given complete access to my trust when something of that nature will influence the Council's choosing?"

Silence stretches between us. I glance behind him, taking in the small trinkets on the dark mahogany bookcases that dominate the wall behind the desk.

"Matching can take years," I say after a while, reiterating my point. "How long will you expect me to submit to the Council's whims, *padre*?"

He blows out a breath, the tension falling from him as he leans forward, his shoulders dropping away from his ears and his hands flattening on the envelope.

"You will submit to being a candidate for at least one cycle, *Domenico*," he murmurs, not an ounce of give in his voice. "In exchange, you will have complete access to your trust, and I or Victor can call on you if a situation requires your set of skills. Yes?"

Better than nothing, I suppose. Though Lorenzo is the better fighter, so the odds of them needing to call in my own brutality is slim to none.

I nod once. "Yes, sir."

"Good," he says, twisting to grab something else from the desk. "Now go talk to your *madre*. She has been worried sick with you being gone all week."

I leave the room, closing the door softly behind me. *Mamma* probably has been worried, but my father only ever uses that as a reason to get his sons out of his office sooner rather than later. He brings up *Mamma*? End of conversation.

The grandeur of the house has faded over time, its appeal lessening each time I return. The heavy woods, the over-the-top artwork, the light tile—it's all a symbol of our wealth and our heritage. But no one else in the family seems to care that it was built with literal blood and violence and preying on the vulnerable. That's me, though, the deer among the predators. If deer also have the ability to kill with little remorse—anymore, at least.

I smooth out my face as I near the kitchen, not wanting *Mamma* to see the indecision. She'll take it personally, a mark against her ability to raise sons that want the family legacy.

She's turned away from the doorway, leaning over the stove as she stirs something into a large pot. I tap on the doorframe of the kitchen so I don't surprise her, and she glances over, eyes wide.

"*Domenico*," she says, a smile lighting her face. "I didn't know you were here today. It's Friday, yes?"

"Fridays you make new pasta, *Mamma*. Why wouldn't I be here?"

She rolls her eyes, my attempt at flattery seen for the diversion tactic it is.

"Come, give me a kiss." She urges me over, the spoon still in her hand, and I indulge her, wrapping an arm around her shoulders and ducking so she can kiss my cheek.

"Have you already met with your father, then?" she asks. I pull away from her and lean against the counter, tucking my hands into the pockets of my slacks. When I nod, she makes a sound in her throat that I've come to know as a sign of her frustration. "Well, you haven't slammed the front door yet, so I'm hoping I managed to get him to see some sense. Just because you are an Alpha does not mean you need to submit to the Council. You're more than capable of finding a beautiful Omega on your own."

It's easier to keep my face neutral with my mother.

"You are staying for lunch, yes, *Domenico*?" she asks, filling the silence with little encouragement from me.

"Of course, *Mamma*," I murmur. My phone vibrates, and I push away from the counter. "Let me just take this call for a moment. I'll be back before the food is ready."

She purses her lips but doesn't say anything, and I'm already halfway across the kitchen when I realize it's not one of Father's men calling me for something they need. I step into the small bathroom just down the hall and close the door, flipping the lock as I answer the call.

"Jasper," I say, leaning against the door. "Everything all right?"

"Sorry, yes," he says after a moment's hesitation.

It's not the first time we've chatted since our date on Wednesday, though he seems more embarrassed than the previous time. The sounds of people talking and laughing filter in through the background.

"Oh my god, is that him?" A female voice gushes loud enough that I can hear it. "Tell him he's hot!"

I chuckle and close my eyes, letting the overbearing feel of my parents' estate fade into the background, too.

"Huntley, I swear to all the gods, shut *up*," Jasper stage whispers.

My chuckle turns into a full laugh. The background din of the call fades before the click of a door closing causes it to quiet entirely.

"Hey, I was just curious what I should expect for Sunday," Jasper says. "And I realize I should have just texted you, but..."

He trails off, and those instincts come roaring to life, wanting to soothe him and make him feel safe.

"It's fine," I say. "My plan is dinner and then letting you turn in the raincheck for that kiss. Though I'm sure I could find a movie or something similar if you want more than dinner."

Jasper chuckles, and my need to see him happy quiets under the sound.

"All right. Cool. Sounds great," he says. I can practically hear him fidgeting.

I put a bit of bite into my voice. "Tell me what's bothering you."

There's a long moment of silence before he blows out a breath. I keep my hand in my pocket, messing with my wallet, forcing myself to be patient.

"It just feels a bit early to be asking what you want from all of this," he says eventually. "But I don't want to have a different idea in my head." I start to say something, but he continues. "Is matching something you really want?"

Translation: Is he just something to pass the time until I find an Omega?

"No," I say, vehement. And it's not a lie. He didn't ask if I plan on matching, only if I want it.

And I don't, no matter what my father is forcing me to do with the Council.

"Oh. All right." The door opens, and noise filters back in. Jasper's voice grows lighter. "So dinner? How fancy?"

"Business casual," I offer.

"Great," he says. That woman says something in the background again, but I choose to ignore it. "I'll be ready, then."

Eight

JASPER

"Oh my God, there you are!" Huntley jumps up from her spot at the table in the middle of the room, grabbing me and pulling me toward the group congregating with her. "I thought you decided to ghost us as soon as we all left."

Going out after the Saturday performance is a way of life for most of the philharmonic. Certainly for the low strings. It's a time I enjoy and look forward to.

Except tonight.

I keep my eyes away from the bar, not wanting to see Rylan before I've decided I can actually handle being around him tonight. I'd thought, after the date with Dominic went so well, I wouldn't react to Rylan quite so much. That the forced nearness of my crashing at his place would be less overwhelming. Somehow, it's managed to do the exact opposite. How can I be so enthralled with Dominic and yet so torn and twisted up over a man that hasn't ever noticed me aside from polite discourse over the last couple years? At best, he offers me a small greeting. At worst, he ignores me outright, frowning and scowling any time our eyes accidentally meet during rehearsal.

I drop into one of the brown chairs, leaning back and shoving my hands in my pockets to keep from fidgeting with my hair. If Huntley hasn't figured out I'm a mess this week, my nervous tick will be sure to give me away. Liz and Mason take pictures across from me, messing with their hair and adjusting how they're sitting to get a different background. Huntley laughs and passes me a tumbler full of amber-colored liquid.

"Got it when we got here. Didn't realize you'd be so long," she explains with a shoulder shove. She blows out a breath as she sits down next to me, swirling the straw in her cocktail and staring at me with far too much intensity. I murmur a small thanks and take a sip, appreciating the burn of the whiskey as I force myself to take in the bar around me.

It's not the one we typically choose as a group. The lights are low, the walls painted a deep forest green. Various bicycle memorabilia decorate the space, large wooden-spoked wheels taking up significant portions of the walls without making it feel cluttered or overbearing. My gaze inevitably lands on Rylan as I take in the space. He leans against the bar top, his legs spread wide, his hair disheveled. He's taken off the flesh-tone neck covering that hides his dual snake tattoo that spreads across his throat and up into his hairline behind his ear. Huntley hums next to me, and I shoot her a look that conveys my feelings over the whole situation.

She, of course, ignores the warning.

"You going to finally talk to him?" she asks before taking a drink.

"I have a second date planned with another man," I say. She raises an eyebrow in silent demand for more information.

If we were anything but Betas, my upcoming second date

wouldn't really matter. Alphas almost always congregate, forming groups naturally. It helps offset the significantly lower occurrence of Omegas—and helps with handling heats, too, I imagine. Instead of only one Alpha to satisfy an Omega, there's two or three or even four sometimes.

But the reality is that we *are* Betas. Sure, there's polyamorous people outside of their designations. But the odds of both of these men being interested in that type of arrangement are low, especially given their opposed views on registering with the Council.

Huntley shakes her head when I stay silent.

"Why does no one else ever notice how stubborn you are?" she asks.

I manage to laugh as I take another sip of my whiskey. "They tend to be blinded by the smile."

Huntley nods. "True. And the blond hair, blue eyes, and body like you're an athlete instead of a cellist don't hurt, either."

"That, too." I smirk and set down the tumbler. The moment of levity is short lived, though, and I'm sighing before I can even help it, my gaze drifting back to Rylan like he's magnetically charged or something. His eyes flick to me for a moment before returning to the other bassist joining him at the bar.

"Dare you to hit on him tonight."

Huntley's words are bold enough that Liz and Mason look up from their phones.

"Who? Hit on who?" Liz asks, leaning forward.

Mason talks over her. "We want to help! You haven't been interested in anyone in *ages*, Jas."

Liz's phone flashes with a message, but she flips it over as she purses her lips.

"We need to do it now," she says. "The guys are going to be here soon, and God knows they'll make it a big deal. They're convinced they're matchmakers now after the gala."

Huntley shakes her head, getting distracted. "As if they're the ones that actually got you guys put together."

Liz nods and twists in her seat. I don't realize what she's doing in time to deflect my gaze from Rylan.

"Oh, seriously?" she gasps, practically vibrating in her seat, her phone and drink forgotten. "Yes, you have to hit on him. He'd probably die of shock and then make out with you right here in the bar."

I scoff and roll my eyes. "You have no idea what he would do."

"Yes, we do," Mason says, his tone matter-of-fact. He takes another drink from the clear cocktail in front of him. "Just because you're blind doesn't mean the rest of us are, Jasper."

I lean forward, resting my forearms on the table, setting my tumbler down.

"What do you mean I'm blind?"

Huntley elbows me in the side. "We mean he's totally into you. Has been since you joined."

I shake my head. "No way. I would have noticed."

All three of them snort and dissolve into laughter.

"Sure, Jas," Huntley says. "You definitely weren't a moping pile of heartbreak when you first joined and would have absolutely noticed someone flirting with you."

"Oh my gosh, yes," Mason gushes before taking a long drink. "So glad you smile now. And laugh. And joke. And—"

I grunt and take another drink of the whiskey Huntley got for me. "I get it, Mason."

His cheeks flush, but he doesn't apologize.

"All right." Liz claps her hands together and grins. "What's the plan, then? You want something more traditional and in the open? Or maybe a bit more covert?"

I tip my head back and stare at the ceiling, slinging the rest of the alcohol in one large gulp.

"Covert for sure," Mason says. "I bet I can get him sequestered near the bathrooms. It would give you a couple moments of seclusion to see what might happen."

I love my friends, but sometimes I wish they'd just fuck off.

"Yes, perfect!" Huntley doubles down, and I know I'm going to lose.

Best to just not fight it when they all get like this.

Liz giggles. "Go, then! There needs to be enough of a gap between you both heading that way for it to not be suspicious. Give us a few minutes before coming back out, too."

I don't even bother fighting, dumping my empty tumbler on the table and rising from my chair. Huntley grins, her eyes too keen, as I head toward the hallway that leads to the bathrooms. It's darker than our typical spot, a small alcove seemingly designed for small little moments like what my friends are trying to develop for me.

Do I even want it though? What good will forced interaction do if all our other interactions have been haphazard at best?

It doesn't take long for my friends to work whatever magic I swear they wield, my thoughts dropping away. Only a couple minutes later, Rylan walks toward where I'm perched with one leg propped on the wall, playing on my phone.

"Oh shit, sorry," he murmurs, edging around me.

I don't manage to move quite fast enough, and our chests brush. A growl rumbles through his chest.

"Fuck me," he mutters. He runs his hands through his hair but doesn't step away from me. Our eyes catch, that same look blazing in his—something nearly akin to *longing* making them sharper. I run my tongue over my lip, trying to figure out what to say, how to make a move. Do I even want to make a move? The whiskey's starting to affect me, my thoughts going a bit hazy at the edges.

I lean forward before I can think better of it, pressing my lips to his. It's like something in him snaps. He grabs my hips and pulls me toward him, our chests flush against each other. I can't quite manage to hold in the groan, and he smirks against my mouth before tracing my lip with his tongue.

"Oh shit, sorry." Another man stumbles into Rylan as he leaves the bathroom.

Rylan pulls away from me, putting enough distance that the kiss almost feels like a dream. His cheekbones are sharp, his eyes dark and hooded.

Liz's Alpha catches my gaze, completely unaware of what's happening between Rylan and me.

"Oh hey, Jasper," he says. "Long time no see. How have you been? Liz mentioned you're seeing someone tomorrow."

Zach moves around Rylan, holding out his hand. I offer a small nod as I take it. Instead of dropping it, he pulls me in for a fast hug.

"She said his name was Donald, I think?"

I can't help but laugh. Of course Liz didn't get his name right. "Dominic."

Zach nods. "Makes way more sense. I couldn't figure out why an Italian would be named Donald, to be honest. Well, I hope you have a good time!"

He walks away, heading back into the bar. I turn toward Rylan, trying to figure out if I should salvage whatever was happening.

The door to the bathroom hinges shut, a flash of Rylan's wavy black hair catching my attention before I'm left in the hallway alone.

Well shit.

Nine

RYLAN

My phone flashes with another text.

I blow out a breath as I ease into the parking space and turn off the car before reaching for it, though I have a pretty good idea of what I'll find. Is it dangerous to be asking Huntley about Jasper's date? Absolutely. She's his best friend, and she sees through me with the same ease the Concertmaster does. The difference? She doesn't hold it over my head the way Ben does.

But desperate times and all that.

His name is Dominic. Why?

And then a second text, just a picture. I drop the phone, not trusting myself to respond.

Dominic. The fucking guy he went on a date with is *Dominic.*

I try not to be melodramatic, but that has got to be some of the most ironic bullshit of my entire fucking life. The man I'm caught up with and completely twisted up over is dating my best friend. It doesn't help that I can still feel the warmth of Jasper's lips on my skin and hear the small noise he'd tried to keep in his throat when I grabbed his hips.

And he's dating fucking *Dominic*.

Dominic, who refuses to register as a pack, would rather throw himself into the ocean than match with an Omega, who has been on a low-dose rut suppressor since I met him in the mandatory designation instruction courses provided by the Council nearly a decade ago.

Tapping the steering wheel, I count back from ten. When I'm nearly certain I won't put my fist into the windshield, I grab the small bag I keep prepped in the back seat and start toward the nondescript building. Alphas are required to use the side entrance, and they don't bother with any kind of aesthethic— simple sliding doors, simple brown awning, a small, tactful sign off to the side marking the entrance. The lobby is the same, sterile tile and white walls broken up by occasional pieces of art.

The pretty stuff is left for the Omegas. They're sensitive to colors, lights, scents. And especially when in heat. Alphas? We don't really give a shit.

A lone desk sits about ten feet into the moderately-sized room. Beyond it, two sets of locked double doors lead deeper into the facility. There's a small waiting area to my left, though no one currently sits there.

A middle-aged man looks up from the book he has perched on the desk, his eyebrow rising as he sets it aside and pulls up something on his computer.

"Are you scheduled, sir?" he asks.

I shake my head as I pull out my Council ID and packet of information. "Not for another few weekends. Wanted to list as available through Monday."

He scans in my information before glancing back at me. "I'll need you to fill out both forms," he says as he grabs a tablet and taps a couple times on it before handing it to me. I work on filling out the information as he gives the standard speech. I tune him out. I shouldn't, but I've done this enough that the speech is memorized.

Don't bond. Don't do anything without the Omega's consent. Pay attention to what the Omega has listed as their preferences. Condoms required if the Omega isn't using birth control regardless of preference.

As soon as I'm finished, he takes the tablet and enters more information into the computer.

"Do you have a preference today?" he asks after a minute.

I shake my head. A minute later, he hands me a packet of information, the paper still warm from the printer, and instructs me to wait for one of the escorts. I flip through the Omega's preference sheet as I settle into a chair, making sure I know the basics before being led to her nest.

The moment I smell her heat, I'll be fucked for common sense and rational thought. My skin already itches with the depth of the Alpha instincts simmering. The key to keeping your fucking wits about you? Make sure you don't let your instincts become so ignored that they become overwhelming. Too bad that's all I've been doing for the last several months while pining after Jasper.

"Ready, sir?" A man about my age stands just behind the chair, his hands tucked into his pockets.

As I stand, I fish my phone out of my pocket and send two quick texts letting Owen and Mark know I'll be unavailable for the next few days. Owen responds within a heartbeat with a thumbs up and polite reminder of Tuesday's rehearsal change. Mark is, unsurprisingly, radio silent. There aren't any gigs scheduled for recording this weekend, so I'm not too worried. I shut my phone off and stash it in the bag before slinging it over my shoulder.

"Yep. Ready."

With a nod, he turns around and leads me across the lobby, pulling a badge from his pocket to unlock the set of doors closest to us. He guides me down several hallways, each becoming more attractive, the cool tile giving way to plush carpet and warm paint. By the time he stops in front of one of the rooms, it feels like we're in a luxury hotel, sconces every few feet lighting the hallway and tasteful decor filling up the empty wall space.

"All needed linens should be in there. If you don't wish to sleep in the nest, there is a key for a separate bedroom just inside the door. She's been asleep for a few hours. This is her first time using the facility."

All information already laid out in the information packet still clutched in my hand. Suppose it's good they double check everything, though. Omegas are especially delicate during their heats. It wouldn't take much for an asshole of an Alpha to really fuck someone up.

I'm an asshole, but never to an Omega.

I stretch my neck and shake my head before rolling back my shoulders.

The moment I open the door, the smell of honeysuckle overwhelms me. The need to rut slams into me, and I grit my teeth to keep it together. I ease into the room and make sure the door latches behind me before grabbing the lone key and heading straight for the spare bedroom. Intent on taking a shower and getting the smells of the bar off of me before it can upset the nest the Omega—Violet—has made, I drop my bag onto the small dresser and strip out of my clothes. The water is quick to heat, and I waste no time getting my skin and hair cleaned with the scent-free options provided by the facility.

I'm towel drying my hair, a set of provided sweats hung low

on my hips, when the sounds change in the other room. There's a whine followed by a hard thud.

"Alpha?" Her voice is tired but strong, and it has a flash of heat racing down my spine.

I focus on the feeling, letting it spread through me, allowing those instincts I keep under a tight leash out to play. Dropping the towel, I cross the extra sleeping room, closing its door quietly behind me as I step into the nest. To keep the need pulsing just behind my sternum and hanging like a haze over my mind from becoming all consuming too soon, I force myself to take in the furnishings she's chosen. Everything has been covered in soft pink and gray linens, pillows in both colors spread across the floor. The nightstand sits at an odd angle, the hard hit I heard from the other room clearly caused by it being pushed over onto its side and hitting the wall.

The Omega's sitting up in the bed, more pink and gray pillows all around her, the plush gray blanket falling and revealing her ample figure and large breasts, her brown nipples tight with arousal. The moment her eyes focus on me, a whine builds in her throat, growing louder with each second. She crawls across the bed, her movements growing more desperate with each second that she's awake and I'm not touching her. Her scent doubles in the room, becoming even more overwhelming, and I let it feed the instinct, let it coax that part of me from where I do my best to keep it hidden without suppressing it. Bergamot blends with her own scent, though I try to ignore it.

"Alpha, please," she begs, splaying her hands on my belly. Her black hair is a mess, falling to her shoulders, her bangs covering her eyes for a moment before she shakes her head.

The need to knot her is strong, the haze fully overtaking me with each lungful of her scent I breathe. I twist my hand into her hair, and she makes a content noise in the back of her throat even as I urge her back onto the bed. She grabs my waist, closing the gap between us. She pants under me, her fingers spasming as she feels my erection press into her soft belly before I adjust our bodies, covering her with my body and settling my hips into the cradle of hers even as she forces my sweats lower. Her fingers shake with the force of her heat despite the information saying she's already been here a full day. Her soft whines build until I push into her, culminating in a sudden moan, her nails scratching my back.

I drop my head into her shoulder and surrender to everything raging through me.

Ten

My phone goes off as I'm adjusting the collar of my button-up, but I pointedly ignore it. The text was sent in a moment of weakness earlier this afternoon when I'd realized Rylan hadn't come home from the bar.

Should I have just minded my own business? Yes. Would it have been better to have texted him directly? Probably. At the very least, it would have saved me from Huntley now breathing down my neck.

The downside to your friend being in all the symphony's business is that she's *in all of the damn business.*

I let the message sit unopened and go through the steps of finishing getting ready, layering my favorite cologne before running my hands through my hair, taming the wild waves without actually worrying about styling it. As I turn to grab my wallet, the light glints off the necklace laying across the top of the small dresser. Another item I really shouldn't have anymore—though at least the hoodie is a culmination of my own decisions.

The necklace? It's just the knife twisted into my side I can't quite manage to pull free. The small Omega symbol spins as I grab the silver chain. I don't bother reading the inscription before hooking it around my neck and tucking the pendant under my shirt.

I gather up my wallet, tucking in two condoms, and head into the living room. Closing the door to my borrowed room, I finally concede defeat and open the message from Huntley.

> He's at the heat facility downtown.
> Apparently he's registered there and works
> on a part-time gig type basis.

> Not totally sure how that works. But Owen is
> certain.

He's a registered Alpha with the Haven?

That's what he must have meant by his registration with the Council that had to be updated every few months. And Owen would know, since he's the principal double bassist. Anything that could jeopardize Rylan being able to attend a concert would need to be cleared through him.

Another message flashes across the screen, and I blow out a breath, forcing the incessant worry down until it's no longer a hulking weight against my chest.

> Finding parking. Give me a few.

> Don't worry about it. I'll meet you out front.

> All right.

Shutting off the lights, I flip my phone to silent and pop another breath mint just in case. I tuck my keys into my pocket and head toward the front of the building, not bothering with the elevator. The two flights of stairs help calm my nerves, but I still run my hands through my hair twice before stepping into the fading sunlight.

Dominic's car is larger this time but no less flashy—a sleek black Alfa Romeo pulled up to the curb outside the apartment building. My date rolls down the window, a half-smile curling his lip. My stomach flips, but I manage to not miss a step, shoving my hands into my pockets to keep from fidgeting.

The moment I've dropped into the passenger seat, he slips a hand around my wrist and pulls me toward him. His lips are soft but unrelenting, and I'm panting within moments, my dick pressing against the zipper of my slacks.

"Hello to you, too," I murmur once he releases me. I can't help but grin, and he laughs. The sound is low in his throat and runs over me like an electric current.

Definitely using that raincheck.

He pulls away from the curb and eases back into traffic, his movements sure. Once we're headed deeper into LA toward downtown, he adjusts his hands so that one rests on my mid-thigh, just high enough to be a claiming move. Heat races across my skin, and I force a deep breath to keep from doing something ridiculous this early on in the night. I cast around for something to say.

"Not heading toward the beach tonight?"

He shakes his head. "Hate the sand. And the people."

Interesting.

Before I can say anything else, he continues, his voice a low murmur. "I thought I'd show you one of my favorite places to eat when my family is too overbearing."

The lifeline is easy to spot, but I take it anyway. "How often is that?"

"More than my mother would like," he says, a small smile

lifting his lips. The near smirk has me shifting in my seat, but I don't look away. "What about yours?"

"They're in Seattle," I say. "I see them about twice a year if I'm lucky. Sometimes I miss them. Mostly I'm glad they're out of my hair."

My mom is the sweetest person in the world. But my younger brother? I could do without him most of the time. He nods as he pulls up to the curb. A young man probably still in college hurries to his side of the car, his simple slacks and vest uniform marking him as a valet. It's nearly identical to the outfit I chose. I glance down at my understated gray suit and second guess my decision. Maybe Dominic's definition of business casual is different from my own. Dominic's hand tightens on my thigh, and I breathe a fraction easier.

Alphas. The thought lands somewhere between grateful and exasperated.

He hands off the keys to the man and then walks around the front of the car. Blowing out a breath, I step out of the car and join him on the sidewalk, running a hand through my hair to try and ease the nerves. It's only the second date, for crying out loud. No reason for me to be this anxious about what might happen at the end of it and especially not next week.

He doesn't want to match, I remind myself. *Just enjoy yourself.*

Easier said than done, but I blow out a breath anyway.

"Jasper?" Dominic's baritone cuts through my thoughts. "*Stai bene?*"

Italian?

For some reason, it surprises me.

"I'm fine, sorry," I murmur. He nods, and we walk into the restaurant, my hands shoved into my pockets to keep from fidgeting.

The hostess looks up from her tablet as the door closes

behind us. Her eyes widen for a heartbeat before she controls her reaction.

"Mr. Gallo?"

"Hello, Sarah," Dominic says, a warmth in his voice I haven't heard much before. "I called ahead this time, I promise."

She nods and scrolls through the tablet, her hands trembling a little.

"My open table is with Darius. Is that all right?" She keeps her gaze on the tablet as she asks.

Dominic stiffens. In the span of a heartbeat, the scent of sour grapefruit permeates around us. Sarah's throat ripples with her swallow.

Wait. Citrus was what I smelled when he scented for me on our first date. Why is he so reactive to the idea of this Darius being our waiter? I keep my body relaxed. I press my hand to the small of Dominic's back and answer for us before something happens that gets us kicked out.

"We'll make it work."

Dominic sucks in a harsh breath and grabs my hand, lacing our fingers together.

Sarah nods and grabs two menus before turning on her heel and heading deeper into the dark, muted restaurant.

"*Mi dispiace*, Sarah," Dominic says once we're seated at a small table in the back corner of the restaurant, tucked away from most of the other patrons. She nods and visibly relaxes, the tension in her shoulders lessening.

There's a level of familiarity that goes beyond him going to this restaurant often. She fills our glasses with water and returns with a small basket of rolls, her movements becoming more steady with each passing moment.

"*Grazie*," Dominic says in a low voice that has even my skin sizzling. She flushes but doesn't look at him.

"Darius should be out in a few minutes," she says before

spinning around and heading back to her post at the front of the restaurant. She's gone before I can offer my own gratitude.

"She's my little sister's best friend," Dominic offers without my asking. "And just recently designated as an Omega."

I resist the urge to look over my shoulder to catch a glimpse of her.

"Isn't she a little... late to designate?" I ask. I'm not the best with guessing ages, but I'd put money on her being the same age as the valet out front. Most people designate as Omega by the time they turn eighteen.

He nods and leans back in his chair. His fingers are sure as he undoes the buttons of his suit jacket and then rolls up the sleeves of his dress shirt.

Shit, that shouldn't do things to me, but another flash of heat races through me, and I force a swallow.

"It helps that Alessia is also an Omega, but, yes, it's been... an adjustment for her." He tilts his head when he finishes rolling his sleeves to his elbows, a thoughtful look crossing his face. "I perhaps should not have soothed her so intensely. But Darius and I... do not see eye to eye. I did not want her to spend the evening worried over what might happen."

Eleven

DOMINIC

"You seriously don't enjoy the beach?" Jasper's eyes are wide as he looks up at me, his fork caught in midair as he pauses his absolute annihilation of the cheesecake Darius dropped off a few minutes ago. "How can you live here and not at least kind of like it?"

He's draped his suit jacket across the back of his chair and undone the top two buttons of his shirt. His smooth, pale skin disappears into the shirt, but I keep finding myself dropping my gaze to the hollow of his throat.

I want to mark him. Even knowing I can't do that—that the only way a Beta can be bonded is through an Omega—the desire rides me hard. I force myself to focus on the conversation.

"I've lived here my whole life," I explain with a shrug, taking a small bite of the chocolate cake Darius had brought me. It's my favorite part of coming here. "I imagine it's similar to people who live in the Rockies and detest skiing."

He leans back, his gaze growing softer. "I'm glad I didn't

suggest the pier as a first date, then," he says. "I imagine that would not have gone as well as the arcade bar."

I offer a half-smile and shake my head. "Probably not," I agree.

"So no beaches. Next you're going to tell me you don't like puppies or something," he says.

"Dogs are fine." I keep my voice dry as I set my fork on the empty plate and push it to the edge of the table. "The larger the better, though. If it jumps when it barks, I don't consider it a dog."

He tosses his head back as he laughs, the low lighting the restaurant uses to create a sense of intimacy highlighting his sharp cheekbones and elegant neck. An image of his throat constricting around my dick has me leaning forward and adjusting how I'm sitting before he can notice.

"I can live with that," he says before taking the last bite of cheesecake. His gaze turns thoughtful. "What about children?"

I shake my head.

"I'd rather deal with the pier," I say with a grimace.

He nods again. His posture is still relaxed, his eyes soft as he pushes the plate toward the edge of the table in mirror of my own. He licks his lips, and it's all I can do to keep from purring. Even still, I scent, the unmistakeable citrus nearly overbearing in the small corner of the restaurant. His lips quirk up.

"Do I still have a rain check?" he asks after a minute.

I have cash on the table and my hand held out to him before he can say anything else. He laughs as he takes my offered hand, and I pull him into me. The kiss is deep and slow, and I groan into his mouth as I cup the back of his neck to keep him close.

Someone clears their throat, and Jasper pulls away from me. The growl rips through me before I even see the person who interrupted us. Darius stands just behind us, his arms crossed, a frown pulling on the small scar on his left cheek. His eyes are hard, his jaw clenched. He isn't at all put off by my territorial behavior. Jasper, though, threads his fingers through mine and murmurs an apology.

"Have a good night, sir," Jasper says.

Darius nods without moving. The air thickens between us, and not in the fun way. His lips curl back, a low growl rumbling through his chest. The smell of roses is offset by the withering tang of his anger. Heat flashes through me, the rage settling under my skin like an old friend. I take a step away from my date, matching the other Alpha's snarl.

"Dominic," Jasper whispers, his voice a soothing balm to the white hot fury whipping my chest.

I force a deep breath, and Jasper squeezes my hand. I allow him to pull me through the restaurant, not dropping my gaze from Darius until we've passed Sarah where she still stands near the entrance. Jasper offers her a soft goodbye, his hand tightening on mine in a universal request for silence.

Once the night air—clean and fresh and just this side of cool —hits me, I suck in a hard, fast breath. Goosebumps race up my arm from where Jasper trails his touch, his hand still laced with my own.

"You all right?" he asks. He's so calm, it sets me back on my heels. Did he spend his down time dealing with touchy, enraged Alphas? God knows the Council doesn't teach Betas anything— despite it probably being in everyone's best interest if they had at least a passing understanding of how to handle Alphas... and probably Omegas, too.

I shove the thought back before I make an even larger ass of myself tonight.

Accidenti.

"*Sì, sto bene,*" I mutter.

Jasper raises an eyebrow and squeezes my hand again. "You sure?"

I tilt my head, focusing on him instead of the cool night that's settled in while we were dining.

"*Parli Italiano?*"

He shakes his head and his cheeks darken with a fast rising blush. "Not really. Just studied enough classical music to have a passing understanding. You go much faster, and I won't know anything."

The young man that had taken the car comes up to us, the keys in his outstretched hand.

"Here you are, sir," he says.

I hand him a larger bill than necessary as I murmur my thanks. Jasper tightens his hold on my hand, and I smile as I guide him to the car, opening the passenger door for him. He raises that eyebrow again but doesn't say anything as I round the car and slide into my own seat. There's no way in hell I'm going to take him in my car. At least not in this particular parking lot. I have everything I'd need stashed in the glove box, but beds— along with couches, chairs, and counters—are much more comfortable than the cramped back seat.

The vision of Jasper bent over my kitchen counter is enough to have my dick hard and aching. Citrus overwhelms the small car, overriding the suppressor, but I do my best to ignore it. My hard-on is more difficult to ignore, but I manage for the sake of the evening. Jasper's throat moves with his swallow, and he messes with a thin chain around his neck.

My carefully crafted plan is thrown out the window the moment he grabs my thigh, his thumb tracing the outer edge of my knee. The touch shouldn't be so consuming, but it's like dousing a fire in gasoline. I grunt and turn at the next light, following the darkened road on the far side of my father's estate. Jasper doesn't say anything, but his grip tightens, and he shifts in his seat, his other hand adjusting his own dick. I pull to the side of the twisting road when I spot the double willow trees that mark the beginning of my own land.

"Think you can fit up here?" Jasper asks, chuckling. His voice is breathless, though, a thread of heat weaving through it. "Or should we just accept defeat and move to the back?"

"Adjust the seat," I order before getting out of the car and walking around the front to his side.

I keep my steps measured. Even with the suppressors, those primitive instincts ride me hard on occasion. And this is one of those occasions. The need to have Jasper's skin under my tongue is almost enough to have the haze of a rut fogging my mind. I bite the inside of my cheek to clear it before opening his door.

With the seat adjusted as far back as it will go, there's just enough room for me to kneel between his spread legs.

Jasper laughs and runs his hands through my hair. "How did you actually manage that?"

I raise an eyebrow and smirk. "Highly motivated," I mutter.

"Fair enough," he says. He buries his hands in my hair and pulls me toward him, his lips demanding against my own. I press into him and run my hands down his chest, undoing the buttons of his shirt as I go. His skin is smooth and flawless, and I don't restrain the urge to mark him, pulling small bits of his skin between my teeth until they bruise.

"May I go higher?"

Jasper nods.

I run my lips across his collar bone, smirking against his skin as he shudders out a breath. He arches up into me when I bite down, bruising the skin just beside the hollow of his throat. I undo the button of his slacks but then pause, waiting for him to signal he's fine with moving forward. Rain check or not, I want to make sure he's as into this as I am. He arches into me, pressing the hard line of his cock into my palm.

I chuckle as I undo the zipper and pull his length out, stroking him from root to tip and back. His cock is as flawless as the rest of him, and my mouth fucking *waters*. He bites out a curse as my lips surround his head and I run my thumb over the thick vein running the underside. Citrus overwhelms the car, so thick I'm practically choking on it, but it doesn't irritate me nearly as much as typical. I relax my throat and take Jasper deeper, locking my gaze with his.

His cheeks are flushed a gorgeous red, his hands twisting into my hair and his feet moving along the floor, like he's trying to stay still but can't quite manage. He arches up, forcing himself deeper, groaning when I don't resist him. I let my hands roam as my mouth continues to work him into a frenzy, the calluses of my fingers catching on the smooth, soft skin of his abs before trailing down his hip bones.

"Shit," he mutters. "Dominic."

It's all the warning I need. He tightens his hold, trying to pull me away, but I take him deeper still, swallowing around his head, forcing him to the back of my throat. His strangled, half-breath groan is my reward. Then his cock twitches against my tongue, and I'm met with the salty tang of his cum.

"Holy hell," he mutters, thrusting into me as the last waves of his orgasm ripple through him.

He pulls me up his body, not bothering to even tuck himself away, and then his tongue is twisting with mine.

"My turn," he says against my lips, a giddy sort of promise lacing the words, and I smirk.

The vibrating of my phone cuts us off before we can decide how to switch positions.

"*Cazzo*," I say. He releases me, and I sit back on my heels.

It's nearly midnight. The only people that call this late are family—and people who need me to clean up after them.

My father's information fills this screen. I tap out a quick text and then stash my phone again.

"Work?" he asks, his gaze full of understanding.

When I nod, he blows out a breath. "I can call a ride share if you need."

I cut him off with a kiss. "It'll keep long enough for me to take you home."

He trails his hands down my chest, tracing the buttons of my shirt. His kiss is slower than mine, deep and sensual. It has my dick aching, practically weeping from knowing it won't get any attention tonight. My father calling this late only means one thing: something went sideways.

"I want another rain check," Jasper whispers against his mouth. "I hate leaving the scales uneven."

I can't help but laugh. "All right, *Tesoro*."

The endearment slips out, and a questioning look crosses his face, but I ignore it, opting instead to help him get his dick put away and his shirt mostly fixed. Once he's resettled, I move back to my own seat.

"And not in a car next time," he says.

My cock twitches, and I run my hand up his thigh. "Sounds good to me."

Twelve

RYLAN

I do my best to ignore Jasper as he prepares a simple breakfast. Just like I do my best to not think about him walking into the apartment in the middle of the night, smelling of Dominic so strongly I could still smell the citrus scent of my friend when I grabbed a drink this morning. Instead, I try to focus on the travel guitar in my hands, running through the extended solo of one of the songs the band is recording tonight. Not that I succeed.

Every few heartbeats, I glance across the open space, watching as he works in the kitchen, my eyes unerringly finding the source of my frustration. This time is no different. The bruise might as well have a spotlight on it, the way it sits above the collar of his black tee but below his hairline. Every Alpha instinct comes surging to life, the need to stake my claim on him, *mark him*, making my hands tremble.

What is it about him that makes me so reactive?

He has no scent, no need for comfort or reassurance, no drive to make me proud or content. He isn't misdesignated. Jasper is as Beta as they come.

And yet I want to bend him over the island and bite over that damn hickey until it's *my* bruise left on his throat. Until it's *my* cock he's stretching his lips around and *my* cum coating his throat. My forgotten boner rages to life at the thought, and it's the metaphorical last straw.

I perch the guitar against the side of the couch and cross the space before he's finished plating the eggs. His head snaps up when I pull the plate away from him and set it on the counter, his eyes wide with his shock. His throat moves with his sudden swallow.

Fuck me, bergamot floods the space. For a moment, I hope he won't notice my scenting, but then his nostrils flare.

"What's wrong?" he asks.

Wrong? Part of me wants to double check he understands what scenting is, what it signifies. Alphas don't fucking scent when things are *wrong*. And right now? The only thing wrong is that I'm pining over a man who clearly has eyes for everyone but me. Including my best fucking friend. I breathe through my nose, clenching my hands, trying to calm that innate part of me that needs him to understand that he's *mine*.

Jasper grabs the edge of the counter, his grip tight enough that his knuckles whiten and his forearms go taut. He runs his tongue over his bottom lip, eyes skating over me. I take another deep breath, trying to convince myself to take a step back, to ignore that hickey, but just as I'm managing to lift my foot, I notice a second bruise just under his left ear, like where I might put a bonding mark on an Omega.

My dick twitches.

"Rylan?" he asks, lowering his voice. It sluices over me, trying to calm me, but all I can think of is someone else—another fucking *Alpha*—having him splayed out on a bed to do with as they please. "What happened, Rylan? What has you so reactive?"

The last bit of resistance fades, slammed out of me by a roaring wave of Alpha-fueled need. I close the distance between us, pressing my hips to his, a growl settling low in my throat. His eyes flare, his hold on the counter relaxing.

"You," I mutter.

I grab him, cupping his face, and slam my lips to his, using my extra inches of height to tilt him to an angle that allows me better access. It's nothing like what a first kiss should be, soft and sweet and unspoken promises. I'm rough and demanding, dumping all my frustration into the movement of my mouth and lips and tongue. He hums, opening for me before I even run my tongue along his lip, and I smirk against his mouth, twisting my hand into the hair at the nape of his neck. I scent harder, bergamot overwhelming the room, so thick I'm practically choking on it. A Beta would probably assume an Omega lives here, it's so powerful in this moment.

His hands are warm where they reach under my shirt and press against my stomach, the calluses from his daily playing catching on my skin. I crowd into him, stealing the last bits of space between us until his breath catches, and then rip my mouth from his, sucking on that damn bruise under his ear, pulling the skin between my teeth.

His groan sets me aflame, a low purr kicking up in my chest that I quickly tamp down. Last thing I need is him knowing just what the hell he does to me. He runs a finger across the waistband of my sweats, the question unspoken but loud enough. I bite that bruise again.

"Is that a yes?" he asks, groaning again as I grind against him.

I nod, running my tongue across his jaw until I see the other hickey. His hands are sure, diving into my pants and circling the root of my cock before I can manage to take a breath. He strokes me, from root to tip and back. My knees buckle, and I bite that second bruise, giving in to the need pulsing through me to claim him as my own.

I'll regret it the moment whatever the fuck this is ends. The moment he pulls away and remembers he hates me and can't stand my presence, that disinterest will dull his eyes, and I'll hate myself for letting him know just how fucking hard he makes me. But I'm not going to deny that his hands on my dick has me wanting to find an Omega just so I can feel him through a fucking bond.

I capture his mouth again, thrusting into his hold, twisting my hands into the short hairs at the nape of his neck. He manages to push the sweats down to my knees without losing hold of me, and fire licks down my spine. That should absolutely not be such a turn-on but *fuck* am I hard right now.

"Jasper," I whisper against his lips.

He pulls away from me, his eyes bright, his cheeks flushed, his neck roughed up from my mouth. He swipes away the pre-cum beading at the tip of my cock, his thumb playing with my piercing even as he uses his hold as leverage to force me to take a step back. I brace myself for the rejection, for the same speech he gave Poppy when she finally braved asking him out at the beginning of the season a few months ago.

You're a wonderful person. An excellent musician. I'm not interested in anything romantic right now. Believe me when I say it's me and not you.

She had handled it with way more grace than I know I'm capable of. She'd even joined Huntley a couple times for trivia— and sat right next to Jasper all evening without a bit of jealousy poisoning her smile in the pictures the group had shared to social media.

Just the thought has me frowning, though his continued

touch keeps my dick from deflating. Why is he still touching me if he's going to let me down gently?

My hips rock forward without my meaning to. His grip tightens, and I stifle a groan. Silence stretches between us, my gaze catching on the way his tongue lingers on his lip, the way his Adam's apple moves with his quick swallow. I open my mouth, not entirely sure what's about to fall from my lips, when Jasper drops to his knees. The movement's so graceful a flash of envy races through me. If I hadn't heard the magic he can pull from a cello, I'd think he'd wasted his potential by not pursuing some kind of sport.

His eyes flicker up to mine, the blue peeking out from his lashes, and my cock twitches in his grip. He doesn't say anything as he takes me into his mouth, his lips stretching, his cheeks hollowing out as he sucks me deep. I lean forward, grabbing the edge of the counter, grunting as he shallows out, his tongue running over the slit, licking away another bead of pre-cum before tracing the piercing with an experimental touch.

The entire time, his gaze stays locked on mine. It's arguably the hottest experience I've had. His soft touch on my thighs sends a shiver down my spine, and I suck in a harsh breath, trying to rein in what I can of the overwhelming rut instinct. I'm only moderately successful, managing to keep from thrusting forward even while I moan, goosebumps racing across my hips as he finds the sensitive space between my dick and my balls.

It distracts me enough that I don't realize how deep he's taking me. I clench my teeth, but I can't keep my growl back this time, the low rumble filling the room as throughly as my scent as I bump the back of his throat.

"*Fuck.*"

The curse falls from my lips, nearly a pained gasp as the muscles of his throat constrict around me, pulling me even deeper, his nose brushing my pelvis. Fire licks through my veins, pooling at the base of my spine.

Because of fucking *course* it would be Jasper that gives such a perfect blowjob that I'm at risk of blowing within three minutes.

The single word admission spurs him on, his gaze trained on me as he works me with a precision I hadn't realized I desire. Sloppy, messy, brutal blowjobs are almost always what I receive, and I luxuriate in them—in the submission they require.

But Jasper's skilled touch has me dangling over the precipice way faster than normal, has me already aching for more. His hands are steady, soft, his lips firm, his mouth the hottest of hells and the sweetest of tortures. Holding back the desire to rut shatters my control, and my release races through me before I can do more than offer a low grunt in warning. Jasper doesn't even blink, swallowing before I've fully spent, his throat squeezing the head of my dick so thoroughly I moan, the sound as breathless and shaky as I feel.

"Jasper," I whisper, the awkward reality of our dynamic creeping back into the room. He pops off me, the slurping sound making me grunt, and then pulls my sweats back over my hips.

"Better?" he asks, still kneeling before me.

When I nod, his throat ripples, and another rush of desire races through me, making my dick twitch again already. He blows out a breath, easing to his feet. I drop my hands, giving him space.

"I have to go."

No.

I grab his wrist as he moves past me, forcing him to still. Something passes over his face, an emotion I don't know him well enough to understand. In a moment, it's gone, his carefree half-smile twisting his lips but not reaching his eyes.

"I have private lessons today," he says, that same careful calm as earlier.

It's like he can tell whatever is upsetting me hasn't really resolved. How the hell is he so attuned to me? Is it because he's fucked Alphas before?

I slam a wall around that thought, beating it to silence. Thinking like that will set me off again. I force myself to release him, watching him the entire time he organizes his things and slings his cello over his shoulders.

"Jasper," I whisper when he's a moment from leaving.

His hand stills on the doorknob, his head tilted away from me. His shoulders move with his deep breath, his knuckles whitening for a hair's breadth of time before they relax again. His voice is soft, careful, but it does nothing to soothe my rage, my primal need for him.

"It doesn't need to change anything, Rylan. I don't expect anything."

Change nothing? He can just give me the best goddamn blowjob of my life and walk away like it was any other typical morning? Like he manages angry, territorial Alphas all the damn time?

A wave of primal need rises in me, so swift it steals my breath. I take a step toward him, but he's already opening the door and stepping out into the hallway. He doesn't look back as the latch resettles. I run my hands down my face as I turn away from the rejection, my skin crawling. His uneaten eggs sit as a silent reminder on the counter. I don't even realize what I'm doing until I hear the shattering of the ceramic against the tile backsplash.

It does nothing to soothe the ache in my chest.

Thirteen

JASPER

"You have got to be *joking*." Huntley stops and spins around, her eyes wide. The bag on her back slaps against the wooden railing. "Please tell me you're joking."

I give her my best unimpressed stare and tuck my hands into the pockets of my jeans. A bicyclist rides between us, offering a short apology without slowing down. Grabbing Huntley's hand, I guide her down the stairs of the pier.

"Oh no you don't," she says, stopping on the first stair. "You are not going to use the beach as a way to distract me from this."

She crosses her arms and leans against the railing, and I tilt my head back, forcing a swallow to try and alleviate the heavy lump taking up most of my throat. Not even two hours ago, it was Rylan making me swallow. I can still feel the phantom press of the metal piercing against my tongue.

I force the thought away, not needing my body to get involved any more than it already has.

"He actually made a move, and you said you had *lessons* today?" Huntley doubles down, despite it being clear I don't want to talk about it. I shouldn't have brought it up at all except she looked at me with that *look*, and I knew it was going to be an uphill battle to convince her to just let me sulk in peace.

"I panicked, okay?" I run my hands through my hair before messing with my necklace. "It was all instinct. I've never seen an Alpha so up in a rage when there wasn't an Omega involved somehow. It started with a kiss and just... just happened, Huntley."

"So he obviously liked it," she says.

I cut her off before she can get some twisted idea in her head. "He wants to register with the Council."

She shrugs. "He already is, right? He works part time at the heat facility downtown."

How she manages to know everything about our coworkers still amazes me.

I shake my head and start down the stairs. I need the sand just as much as she does today. Huntley sighs, but I hear her footsteps a half-stride behind mine.

"Is there a different way to be registered?" Huntley asks as we get to the bottom of the stairs and head toward our favorite lounge spot. "Because I really only thought there was the one way."

I nod, and she curses under her breath.

"They should really offer classes to Betas," she mumbles.

I don't disagree. A lot of things would be more straightforward if they extended us the same knowledge and education they do to Omegas and Alphas.

Huntley grabs my elbow and forces me to stop. "What way do you mean, then? Why is it something that you feel is insurmountable?"

"He wants to register to be matched." I spit the words out and twist out of her hold, continuing down the beach.

"Oh," she says.

It's an impressive moment, seeing Huntley at a loss for words. It just drives the reality even harder. Rylan is completely out of my reach.

"I shouldn't even be bothered by it. I'm already seeing someone else," I bite out, turning. She stumbles into me, not anticipating my sudden stop. Behind her, a flash of black hair grabs my attention.

No way.

I adjust her, trying to see around the small groupings between us and the ocean. Where had it gone, that flash of hair I knew better than my own? A redheaded woman about Violet's age tosses her head back and laughs, the sun catching on her freckles and a small gold piercing in the upper part of her ear.

"Couldn't you register with him?" Huntley asks, forcing my attention away from where I could have sworn I'd seen Violet.

I twist back to her and sigh. "If I want to continue with Dominic, no. He doesn't want to register."

Huntley's lips twist, and I shrug even as her grimace deepens.

"You like him that much?" she asks. "After avoiding Alphas for years?"

"Yeah, H, I do," I whisper, the admission both freeing and gutting. How could any person, especially a Beta like me, be able to hold such space for two men—two *Alphas*? Omegas are naturally wired for this type of thing. I am not. And yet it's the reality: I desire them both.

Huntley tucks her arm into mine and starts us walking again, leaning her head against my shoulder. "I'm sorry, Jas."

I lean over, resting my head on hers.

"I've never wished to be anything other than I am," she says after a while.

In front of us, the pier stretches into the ocean, the Ferris wheel spinning in its slow jaunt like it has no care in the world. Young kids run around, their laughs audible even over the sound of the tide and the call of the gulls.

"Being a Beta has always just…" She hesitates before shrugging. "It's always made sense to me. I wish I had something to offer you."

I manage a small laugh, though mostly my chest just hurts. "It's all right, H. I didn't really mind not designating until Violet did."

She nods. Her hair scratches against my arm, but I don't say anything.

"I know. But still…" She trails off, and I wrap my arm around her shoulders, offering the world's most awkward side hug since our other arms are still linked. "I'm sorry you feel like you have to choose between parts of you."

I don't have a good answer, so I just give her another awkward hug and let my arm drop, tucking my hand into my pocket. Huntley doesn't let the silence linger for long.

"Invite him to the concert," she says. At my hesitation, she elbows me in the side. "I know you haven't used your friends and family tickets. See if he'll come see you play. And when you guys join us for drinks after, we can see if he's worth the trouble of giving up Rylan."

"I don't think you can call it giving up Rylan when we've never even been a thing," I mutter.

She shakes her head. "You know what I mean, Jas."

I pull out my phone and send the text before I can reason myself into something more safe—and lonely. It's only a few minutes before he replies.

Love to. May I pick you up?

Huntley leans over and giggles. I shove her, pulling my arm free of hers, but she just laughs harder.

"He's just so polite. I really expected him to be more... I don't know. Dominant or something."

I cock an eyebrow, but she's the definition of innocent, her eyes wide and her smile saccharine. I stare at her in unspoken question, knowing she'll break eventually. It doesn't even take a full minute.

"You have never once let your partners leave marks when you won't be able to hide them easily," she says. "And yet I can see three hickeys in full view and another two under your collar when you turn just right."

I can't stop my cheeks from heating, so I focus on responding to Dominic instead.

> I have to report an hour early. You'd end up sitting for a while.

> I don't mind.

> All right.

Huntley stays surprisingly quiet during the exchange, only looking over my arm to see the conversation. Once we've settled on timing, I tuck my phone away and start down the beach again, grabbing Huntley's hand as I head toward our favorite spot. She pulls a blanket from her bag and spreads it on the ground before sitting cross-legged and tilting her head back, a small smile on her lips.

"Don't do anything with him there." I sit next to her, toeing off my sandals in favor of digging my toes into the sand. She gives me an impressive side eye that I don't believe for a minute. She cracks a moment later, shrugging. "Seriously, Huntley. Don't do anything overbearing."

She purses her lips but nods. "Promise."

I lean back on my elbow and close my eyes, settling into the familiar sounds around us. She adjusts to lay her head on my stomach, and I can't help but smile.

Fourteen

DOMINIC

Rylan walks into the café ten minutes late—which is about five later than normal. His eyes are heavy, the circles under them dark, a bruise marring the serpent tattoo on his neck. It screams that he's been out of town, out of his own apartment, though he's freshly showered and in his own clothing. Rylan sleeps like shit anywhere but his own bed.

I wave him over, and he drops into the seat across from me, not waiting for the waitress before trying to steal my own flat white.

"*Vaffanculo,*" I mutter, slapping away his hands. "Order your own."

He growls, low in his throat, his shoulders tensing in a heartbeat. The waitress stills where she stands about five feet away, a water in her hand, her wide eyes flicking between Rylan and me. The rest of the café quiets, the patrons shifting in their seats and the hostess messing with the menus to keep from being obvious in her eavesdropping.

"Rylan," I murmur, dropping my tone until it barely reaches between us—and certainly doesn't carry to the rest of the tables.

He finally looks up at me, and I mutter a curse that would have my mother smacking my hand. Though she'd smack me for telling someone to fuck off, too. I allow him to take the coffee and nod to the waitress. She turns on her heel and disappears toward the kitchen with hurried steps.

"Who the hell set you off?" I bypass any niceties. "You look like shit, *amico*."

He takes a long drink of the coffee, closing his eyes and breathing deeply. "Fuck off, Dom."

His eyes flash in warning, and I lean back in the booth. He doesn't want to talk about whatever Omega has him riding the line of control so hard right now? Fine. This is why I take a rut suppressor, for fuck's sake.

The waitress sets a new flat white in front of me, and I offer a small order for the both of us, not trusting Rylan to behave himself if he's already so worked up. The rest of the cafe slowly returns to normal, and I relax into my seat, biting back my own questions so that Rylan can find some semblance of calm. The hostess glances toward us. I offer a subtle shake of my head before Rylan looks up from the coffee.

"What's up?" Rylan breaks the silence eventually.

"I need help."

That pulls him from wherever his thoughts are. His eyes flick up to mine, his gaze sharpening as he actually looks at me.

"You never need my help," he says after a minute. His fingers tap on the small mug. "What the hell did you get yourself into that you need me? Can't one of your brothers bail you out?"

I shake my head. "It's a problem with my father," I mutter and lean forward.

The second cup of coffee isn't as well-balanced as the first, probably from the waitress's nerves. I set the mug down after a small sip, holding back my grimace.

Rylan mutters an apology and switches the mugs.

"Your father? What the hell does he want?"

"For me to match." Even trying, I can't manage to say it in anything but a snarl.

Rylan tilts his head back and *laughs.*

"*Stronzo,*" I mutter.

He rubs his hands down his face before scratching at the tattoo.

"You have to see the irony here, Dom." He drinks from the new mug, completely unaffected by the imbalance between coffee and milk. "What is he holding over your head that you're actually pissed off by his demand?"

My phone vibrates, but I ignore it for the moment.

"My trust fund," I say.

Rylan doesn't miss a beat. "Fuck, yeah, that would do it." He shifts forward, leaning on his elbows and raking his fingers through his hair. "What exactly are his terms?"

"I'm to submit to attending one gala."

I don't bother to hide my distaste for the entire premise. Is it better than what he'd initially required of me? Yes. Do I still detest it even days later? Absolutely.

Rylan glances up at me. "So you'll need to register with the Council," he says. "You have a plan for that?"

I shrug. "Was hoping you would be interested."

He doesn't immediately agree. My phone vibrates again, so I pull it from my pocket and check to make sure my father doesn't need me. I find a text from Lorenzo about tonight's fights. I ignore it in favor of the text from Jasper.

> Would you like to go to the symphony Saturday? I have a discounted ticket.

Love to. May I pick you up?

"You know I want to be matched," Rylan says, his words cautious. "There's a lot of paperwork involved, though, especially since you'll probably do everything in your power to not get matched that night, anyway. It won't put me in very good standing with the Council."

I set my phone down so I'm not distracted by Jasper.

"I'll make sure it doesn't count against you when you decide to make a more permanent decision," I say. "Victor has a couple of contacts."

He nods but doesn't immediately say anything, his eyes unfocused.

My phone vibrates again, and I take the moment to work out details for the concert with Jasper.

"I don't know of a third person," he says after a while. "It's part of why I haven't registered yet. And finding someone who will be willing to do it only for show? That's even harder to find, I think. There aren't a lot of people who are willing to potentially piss off the Council with a ruse of a pack."

The waitress sets the food between us, and Rylan attacks it with a force that belies his fatigue. Or maybe explains his fatigue, really.

"Thought you didn't have a shift at the Haven this month." I offer the comment in an offhand tone as I dig into my own food. Rylan glares at me without actually looking up from the plate. I can't help but goad him just a bit. "Did he smell nice?"

"She," he corrects through clenched teeth. "And yes. Something floral."

My lips tip up. He must have really liked her to only admit to her scent being floral. God knows he probably knows exactly what flower.

"You are a sucker for floral."

Rylan merely glares again.

Something clicks into place. Fuck me, no wonder he doesn't want to just register for a single gala.

"I thought you were ready to deactivate with the Haven. What changed?"

The plate breaks under the force of his cutting. The couple in the booth behind him flinch, the woman grabbing her throat as she turns toward the sound.

"New pretty Omega flustering you in the symphony?"

He drops the fork and clenches his hands, the veins in his forearms even more pronounced than usual. I'm an asshole for egging him on like this. I never said I was nice, though, especially when it comes to securing my goals.

"If I agree, will you stop asking?" He bites out the question and shoves away the broken plate.

Nearly there. "I bet she's blonde. You're a goddamn sucker for them."

"*He*," Rylan snarls and shoots to his feet, "isn't even an Omega."

There it is.

I take another controlled bite of the food as I watch my friend. His chest heaves and his hands shake, his normally earthy scent carrying the tang of his protective rage. Must be one *hell* of an Alpha to get him so worked up like this.

He blows out a breath and stretches his neck before collapsing back into the seat.

"Want me to put up a profile in the local matching app, then?" he asks. "Or are you being a complete asshat just for fun today?"

I shake my head. "Can't it be both?"

Rylan moves fast enough I don't have time to brace for the hit.

"*Accidenti*," I mutter. I drop into Italian as I shake out my arm. "*Che maledettamente male, stronzo.*"

"Does that mean it hurt? Because I fucking hope it did, Dom. You're being an ass, even for your standards."

I wave him off.

"If I find a third person, will you do it?" I ask.

Rylan doesn't say anything, keeping his gaze locked on mine. The cafe is slower to return to normal. I make a mental note to tell my father I owe the owner for the disruption. He'll be pissed if his favorite place to do business—outside of his office—no longer lets us in.

"You will do everything for it. And you'll have Victor do whatever needs to happen in order for my standing in either regard to not be fucked over because of this." He drains the last of the coffee. "And I'm not finding a third person. Let me know when you've picked someone."

When I nod, he pulls cash and drops it on the table. I don't protest simply because I know it'll soothe that need driving him hard right now—protect, provide, procreate. That's what the Council labels them as. I prefer fight, fawn, and fuck, but to each their own, I suppose.

"I'll let you know if the person I'm thinking of works out," I tell him as he turns away from the table.

His only response is flipping me off.

Fifteen

RYLAN

"How's the roommate?"

One of the studio's audio interns grins as I get both guitars situated. Aaron gets under my skin on the best of days. Between Dominic being an utter asshat at lunch and me still stewing over what happened this morning with Jasper, this is the *opposite* of a good day. The last thing I need is to be in a room alone with Aaron's dumb bullshit right now. I scowl, not controlling the growl that rumbles through my chest.

For once, he seems to have an ounce of self-preservation, leaving the room at not quite a run. *Good.* One more look at his cocky ass smirk, and I'll probably damage something expensive in the booth.

My hands shake as I set about unpacking everything. Forcing my mind to quiet, I sort through my things and organize it all in preparation for the marathon recording session we're about to start for one of the lesser-known pop stars in the area. I'm just finishing adjusting my pedal set-up when Mark walks through the door, a frown already set on his face.

"What's up?" I ask the audio engineer, twisting around but staying in my crouch.

"Change of plans from the record label. They want the third song to feel more punk than pop."

I raise an eyebrow. "Meaning?"

"You'll need your heavy distortion."

Fuck.

"I'll see if someone can grab it from my place. I didn't bring that pedal."

I try to only bring what I need. Pedals are expensive, that particular one especially. The less I move them around, the less likely they are to be dropped and the more likely they'll survive until the next royalty check comes in.

He nods.

"We'll run through the other songs first, then. I don't want Jonas to be running any type of solo work for this album."

What the hell did Jonas do to piss you off?

I bite back the question as he heads back out of the booth, turning off one of the overhead lights. Instead, I grab my phone from the stool I've claimed as my own for when I'm here. I send a quick text to Liz. She lives closest to the studio, so I'm hoping she has a chance to swing by and grab the keys to get it. Or one of her Alphas, at least.

> On it. Be there soon.

We settle into the rhythm. Unlike most nights we're here, though, I don't quite manage to sink into the music, my body still tense with everything happening outside of the studio. Jonas and Trent are more aware than Aaron, though, and they tread lightly with each spike of my scent—tangy with my barely banked rage—that happens across the playtime. We work through the first two songs before I start to worry that Liz might have gotten distracted. When Mark tells us we're going to move on to the next song, I check my phone for the third time.

"Shit, I think whoever you texted is here, Rylan," Jonas mutters, picking out a half-familiar melody on his simply painted Fender.

His foot pressing the volume pedal to the floor keeps his guitar muted in the monitors, though I pull my in-ears anyway. With a quick glance at the control room, I catch Mark standing and Aaron grinning. I twist, intent on storing my guitar to go greet Liz and hand her my keys when the door to the recording booth opens.

"Hey Huntley," Jonas says, suddenly shy.

I turn fast enough the room spins for a moment. What the hell is Huntley doing here when I texted fucking *Liz*?

"Hey Jonas," she says, her cheeks flushed. Her eyes catch on mine, and she smirks, shrugging before handing me the pedal I needed. "And before you ask, no, I had no idea which one you needed. Jasper grabbed it when Liz texted to see if he was at your place."

Jonas laughs. "Shit, Rylan, were you going to tell the rest of us peasants? That moved fast."

"There's nothing to tell," I snarl, using the pedal as an excuse to turn away from them both.

Jonas reads my voice and backs down, picking that same melody after a moment of hesitation. Huntley, however, just laughs.

"Trust me, Jonas, you'll be one of the first to know if anything actually happens, I'm sure."

Why the hell didn't the Council teach Betas a single damn thing about interacting with Alphas? The last thing I need tonight is to end up in a fucking fist fight with a coworker.

I snap the instrument cable in my hand and toss it aside, breathing heavily through my nose, forcing my hands to stop *fucking* shaking. I cross the room to the small stack of replacements—though they're actually on standby for when more instrumentation is needed.

"You ready to head out?" Jasper leans against the door frame of the studio, his hands tucked into his pockets.

Huntley turns toward him and nods, flipping her hair over her shoulder. "Good to go. I'll get a ride share ordered really quick." She pulls out her phone, tapping on the screen a few times, and then waves to Jonas. "See you later."

Jonas smiles and nods, his hands not faltering on the strings. "You guys still do trivia on Thursdays?"

Huntley nods. "You interested in getting your butt kicked?" she asks, smiling again.

"Jasper won't let me end up on the losing team," Jonas jokes. "He likes me too much to let that happen."

Jasper laughs. I growl. Huntley steps toward Jasper. My growl grows and my hands shake too much to hide them even by stuffing them into my pockets. The room quiets.

Fuck.

"Rylan?" Huntley asks, turning toward me. "You all right?"

Jonas rests his guitar against his legs, moving slowly just within my line of sight. His body is relaxed, but his eyebrows are furrowed and his lips are pulled low into a heavy frown.

"You good, Rylan?"

I shake my head.

Mark's voice slices through the silence of the studio. "Everyone take five. We'll start in on track two of the album when we come back."

Jonas cuts across the room, moving just fast enough to give away his nerves. Huntley brushes past Jasper, and the contact she makes with him has my growl growing deeper. I'm across the room and in front of him before I even realize I've made the choice.

Jasper's gaze is careful, his hands hanging limp at his sides as he straightens and takes a step into the studio.

"You all right?"

His voice is low and calm like this morning. Any other day, and the calming effects of his being a Beta might actually work. But not right now, with the memory of his hands on me and those hickeys still visible on his neck and just under his collar. Not with Dominic's pestering laying me open for him and the reality of what I've agreed to with him hanging over my head.

Dominic couldn't possibly mean to ask Jasper to be the third man, could he? I'd have to back out, tell him to find someone else, some other Alpha. The last week in the apartment has been hell enough for me. No way could I spend another six months living so close to him and expect to remain sane by the end.

"Rylan?" Jasper cuts through my inner panic. "You were fine a few minutes ago."

I shake my head. "I haven't been fine."

"All right." He agrees without fight.

It should soothe me. My eyes lock on the hickey just under his collarbone, and the growl deepens in my chest. The bergamot scent explodes from me, tainted by the sour notes of my rage.

"You okay to keep playing? Mark probably can't afford much longer of a break."

"Yes," I say but shake my head.

Jasper purses his lips. "What set you off?"

The last portion of my rational brain clicks off, all those instincts screaming at me finally winning out.

"You," I grunt. I grab his throat and pull him to me, keeping my thumb and forefinger on the pulse points just under his ears. It hides the hickeys, and part of me calms a fraction.

"That's not possible," he murmurs, though his eyes keep dropping to my lips like he wants to kiss me.

Take that, Dominic.

"Why would it not be possible?" I ask the question to distract myself.

"I'm just a Beta." He says it so plainly, it shocks me to stillness for a moment.

And then I'm slamming my lips to his.

"Does it seem like I care, Jasper?" I mutter the words against his lips, breathing them out even as I breathe him in.

I pull him even closer, forcing him to take a step into me, and then grind against his hips. His hands settle on my waist, his fingers tracing shapes along my sides even as his body stays relaxed against me, completely willing to let me control whatever the fuck this is I'm demanding of us right now. Using my grip on his throat, I push him into the doorway, utilizing every single scrap of the two inches of height difference between us to make sure I crowd over and around him. He melts into me, his tongue exploring with a thoroughness that has a bolt of lightning shooting down my spine and straight into my dick.

There's a soft knock on the door, and Jasper forces the kiss to slow and shallow out. When I open my eyes, I'm confronted with his stark gaze, the unspoken question clear in them.

If he asks, I'll be honest. But to offer anything of what's roiling inside me without prompt? Absolutely not happening.

"Jas?" Huntley's voice is cautious as the door edges open. "Our ride is here."

"Be right out," he says, only a little breathless.

His throat ripples under my palm as he swallows. I force my hands to drop and take a step away, not dropping his gaze. A purr starts low in my chest, and I don't try to hide it. He runs his hand through his hair before messing with a necklace tucked under his shirt.

"I..." He shakes his head. "I don't understand."

He doesn't wait for me to offer anything, say anything. His strides eat up the distance between the studio and the door leading out of the control room. Huntley opens the door wider as he nears her, her brows furrowed as she looks between us. She says something that I can't quite hear, and Jasper shakes his head.

The band is filtering into the room the moment Huntley and Jasper are out of sight, settling back into the feel of recording. Mark takes one look at me and sighs.

"Change of plans. Let's do track seven."

Sixteen

JASPER

The small timer goes off where I've set it on the side table near me. I finish playing through the piece, and then set my cello in its case, grabbing the rosin from the small storage bag. Not even the monotony of tending to my bow is enough to drown out the thoughts entirely.

Thoughts that have been nothing but obnoxious since Monday. I'm about ready to throw everything out and start over.

It worked after Violet.

My phone ringing cuts the idea short. It's not quite as easy to drop everything when you're already part of one of the top philharmonics.

"Mr. Miller? This is Candice with Soltaire Apartments."

The bright voice is in direct odds with my mood, but I force a deep breath. Hopefully she has good news for me.

"How can I help you?" I ask, tucking my phone between my ear and shoulder. I put away my bow and rosin and stash it behind the door of my borrowed bedroom.

"We've just gotten final word from the contractor," the woman says. "The apartment is cleared for move-in starting Tuesday."

I ignore the sinking of my stomach and grab my cello. This is what needs to happen. I go back to my place and my own life. See what this thing with Dominic might turn into. Hang out with my friends. Work my ass off to get principal when Liz's swan song is finished. I knew three years ago when I saw Rylan the first time that there would be nothing but heartache between us.

Realizing I was right doesn't help soothe me, though. I clear my throat.

"Great. Thank you."

She hangs up only a few moments later, the deep rumble of someone talking nearby telling me someone else needs her help. I tuck my phone into my back pocket with a sigh.

I set my cello case next to the one holding my bow and run my hands through my hair. An itchy, antsy wave of nerves settles just under my skin. Grabbing my hoodie, I stride across the apartment and grab my water bottle, taking a long drink before my brain can fully set in with the haphazard, angry thoughts the music had at least dulled. I glance at the clock above the stove and curse. No time to take a run if I'm going to be on time meeting Huntley tonight.

The front door closes with a heavy slam. My phone rings again.

"You hear anything yet?" Huntley asks the question before I've even gotten the phone to my ear.

I watch Rylan unload his things out of the corner of my eye.

"Hi, Huntley, it's nice to hear from you," I say with overdone sweetness.

There's a long pause. Rylan picks up one of the guitars he keeps on stands around the perimeter of the living room. "Did I interrupt something interesting? Wait, don't answer that. I don't want to know if you're one of those assholes that answers your phone in the middle of everything."

"Huntley," I mutter. "What do you need?"

"You still good for tonight?"

Of course I am. If she's double checking with me, something's happened to make her nervous.

"What happened?"

She blows out a breath that I can hear through the phone. Something clinks in the background, like she dropped her keys.

"Jonas asked if he could join."

I raise an eyebrow. "He's come before." Rylan tenses, so I continue. "Why is tonight any different for you?"

"Because Mel doesn't want to go exclusive," Huntley mutters.

"You need me to play buffer? Or wingman?" I lean against the counter of the island, resting my head in my palm.

Huntley hums. "I... don't know. Maybe both?"

"Whatever you need."

"All right. See you soon."

The line clicks dead before I can say anything in return, but that's Huntley when she's stressed out. I take a deep breath and close my eyes, counting to ten. The soft sounds of Rylan finger picking the melody to an old Paramore song surrounds me. I can't help but sink into it, into the feeling that this could be something more than just a temporary experience.

I clear my throat before the enjoyment can morph into longing.

"I got a call about the apartment," I say into the sudden silence his stopping brings the apartment. I turn enough so I can see him.

He frowns and runs his hand along the side of the guitar, messing with the bridge pins.

"It's clear to move back on Tuesday."

I'm not entirely sure what I'm expecting—and in complete denial over what I'm hoping he'll do. His face clears, any emotion gone from his gaze as he looks up from the guitar. His look hits me like a punch to the chest anyway, though, and I have to force myself to breathe through the impact. Shit, if this is how *I* respond, how many Omegas has he brought to their knees?

"All right," he says, his voice as unaffected as his gaze. "I have my own lesson that morning. Do you need me to find someone to help?"

Why am I *disappointed*?

In answer, my mind offers the memory of his lips on mine, his hand on my throat. I shake my head, trying to clear the thoughts. I've had one night stands before, lighthearted hookups that meant even less for me than they did for my partner. So why can I not shake *this* one?

You know why, dumbass.

I ignore the voice nagging at me.

Rylan nods. "Sounds good, then."

He stands in one fluid motion. My stomach clenches and my dick hardens, ignoring my urging.

"About Monday," I start, hesitant.

He freezes, his body turned toward his bedroom. He clenches his hands and takes a deep breath. "What about it?" Even his voice is blank, flat.

Silence stretches between us. Can I really handle him rejecting me? This silence is awful, but it can't be worse than hearing he doesn't really want me, that Monday was just a mess created by him being newly off shift from the Haven. I close my eyes and force myself to find that inner part of me that's faced down conductors with poise and Violet's mother with a saccharine smile.

"Is it something—"

The click of a door cuts me off. My eyes snap open. I drop my head into my hands and ignore the empty room around me.

Seventeen

DOMINIC

"Jasper, over here!"

A short blonde woman waves from across the bar, her grin as bright as her green eyes. Jasper squeezes my hand as he waves back and begins to navigate around the other people standing in groups of three or four. The room itself is dark, the walls a deep midnight blue and covered in polaroids of people in various stages of happiness. The small woman runs up to Jasper when we get close enough.

"You did such a good job tonight," Jasper says with a smile, resting his cheek on the crown of her head.

The woman preens under his praise. I force the instinctual jealousy down before it can ruin the rest of tonight.

"Is this him?" she asks as she steps away, those clear eyes lighting on me. A group of men stand against the back wall, their poses relaxed, but all of them focus on me. The man on the end clenches his jaw as she holds out her hand.

"Hi, I'm Liz. You must be Dominic," she says.

I take her hand in an easy grip before tucking my hands into the pockets of my slacks. "Nice to meet you, Liz."

A low rumble from the men has me cursing under my breath.

Liz blushes before clearing her throat.

"Huntley is getting drinks." She turns to Jasper and points toward the other back corner of the space where a long bar stretches, rows of liquor piled behind the three bartenders doing their best to keep the line from getting out of hand.

"What would you like?" I whisper the question into Jasper's ear, keeping my voice pitched low enough that no one else will hear me.

It's not quick enough to keep the other Alphas from approaching.

"Hey, Jasper," the largest of them says. His mousy brown hair flops onto his forehead, and he shakes it away. The men exchange greetings and handshakes, and Jasper visibly relaxes with each one, his voice warming as the last man offers a greeting.

"Hey, Zach," he says, his voice full of affection. "Glad to see you here. I thought you would be gone again."

Zach shakes his head. "Have another week before I'm due back. And then only six months before I'm out entirely."

Liz trembles where she's tucked under his arm, and he tightens his hold, brushing his lips against her temple. The touch calms her.

Omega.

Well, that explains the jealousy.

"This is Dominic," Jasper says after a half-second too long.

I glance at him, but he's staring at something behind us, toward the front of the bar. I follow his gaze—just in time to see Rylan staring at me, absolute anger etched into the features of his face.

I can't help but egg him on, even now. I wrap an arm around

Jasper's waist and close the distance between us until I feel Jasper plastered against my side.

Rylan's neck flexes, the muscle in his jaw twitching as he clenches his teeth. The man beside him says something, and he shakes his head, leaving cash on the bar and heading outside without looking back.

Liz sighs. "He's been in such a bad mood all week."

She turns a gaze full of questions on Jasper. He blows out a breath and runs a hand through his hair. Before he can say anything, though, I lean into him, making sure my lips touch his ear. I hide my grin as goosebumps rise along his neck.

"Let me get us some drinks," I murmur.

This time, he nods. "Double whiskey, please. On the rocks."

With a nod, I drop my arm and navigate my way across the room, settling into the small line of other people—most of them vaguely familiar from the concert—waiting for their own chance to order something.

A tall woman with shoulder-length brown hair steps up beside me, a touch too close for the current level of crowd the bar was managing. Both hands hold mixed drinks, one pink and one a pale yellow.

"So you're Dominic," she says.

I glance at her, not untucking my hands. "And you are?" I ask, dropping the false niceties that keep others from being intimidated by me.

"I'm Huntley, Jasper's best friend."

Best friend? So why wasn't she there tonight? Especially given that she's dressed similarly to Liz.

"You're part of the orchestra?" I ask.

"Principal Oboe." She offers a half-smile, but her eyes are still calculating. "Most people aren't able to see me while we're performing."

Fair enough.

"Look," she says after a moment.

The bartender waves me forward, and she goes with me, her lips pursed as I order Jasper's request and a Negroni for myself. I hand the woman enough to cover both drinks and a decent tip before taking both drinks and turning away from the bar.

"Hold on," Huntley says, stepping just enough in front of me to keep me from heading back to Jasper. To most people, though, it looks like she just leaned in to say something.

Accidenti.

"Yes?" My voice is barely more than a growl.

"You're friends with one of the bassists, right?" She takes my raised eyebrow as answer enough and continues. "Great. Look. Rylan has had a thing for Jasper since Jasper flew down from Seattle to audition. I don't really know what happened before then, just that Jasper came to that audition with his heart on his sleeve and hope in his eyes. When he joined the orchestra a couple months later, it was with a broken heart."

She flips her hair over her shoulder and steps fully in front of me, encouraging me back toward the bar. Most of me wants to push the issue, to show her what happens when a disrespectful Beta tries to manhandle an Alpha. But the low-dose suppressor takes just enough of the rage away that I'm able to hold my tongue.

"How do you know that? Other performers aren't typically part of auditions."

She nods. "I wasn't part of it. Saw him walking the hallway. And the assistant director at the time was one of my best friends from college. I trust her measurement of a person."

She pauses, waiting for me to press the issue, but I shrug. "All right."

With a nod, she continues. "Rylan has done a damn good job hiding his interest this entire time. Flirted a couple times the first month or so Jasper joined but then stopped. Keeps mostly to himself. I know the orchestra isn't his only job, so most people assume that's why. But you know what I think?"

She takes a breath and continues, not waiting to see if I can—or even want to—answer her rhetorical question.

"I think that Rylan doesn't get along with the Concertmaster. Ben's an asshole to pretty much every Alpha. Not sure why. I don't rock that boat. I like having my place in the symphony, thank you very much."

Jasper looks up and catches my gaze. I give an easy smile, hiding the tension of the moment well enough that he smiles back and turns back to Liz and her Alphas. I take a sip of my Negroni to keep my mouth shut.

"I think that Rylan realizes that most of the orchestra absolutely adore Jasper, though he doesn't seem to see it. I think that Rylan would go after Jasper in a heartbeat if he thought Jasper was truly interested."

Her pause this time is longer, carrying a weight with it.

"You asking me to break up with him?" The question is a snarl.

She pales but doesn't move away.

Points to her.

"I think that you're Rylan's friend."

My eyebrows shoot up.

"My sorority sister works at a small cafe in Brentwood." The information comes out of nowhere, but I hold my tongue, sinking into the training my father and uncle gave me as a teenager. People with information don't always go about giving it in concise ways. Huntley takes a drink from the pink drink. "We make a game of seeing if anyone interesting eats there—normally celebrities and other really famous people. But when Rylan walked in earlier this week, she sent me a text. He doesn't quite fit in, and she knows him from when he used to go to Thursday trivia."

She sighs. I take another drink and look toward Jasper. His shoulders shake as he laughs with the group congregated around Liz. She's radiant, soft and delicate and absolutely not my type. Her grabbing Jasper's hand is enough to drive my jealousy into my voice.

"Your point?" I growl.

Huntley swallows.

"Rylan has been all kinds of caught up with Jasper, and I know them living together these last two weeks hasn't helped with any of that. No, I won't tell you why I know that," she says, not even waiting to see if I'll make an objection. "And I know that Jasper is into him, too. Just like he's clearly into you. I don't know how to get Rylan into this whole thing with you both, but you need to try. Because if it doesn't happen, I don't see how Rylan or Jasper will survive to still be part of the orchestra by the end of the season. Rylan is the best damn bassist we've had in the last ten years regardless of whether Ben wants to admit it. And Jasper is one of the good ones—the ones that help everyone meld together when it's easier for us to get too competitive. I don't want to lose either of them."

I nod, finally understanding what she's asking.

"I know that Jasper's a Beta and not an Omega, so maybe it's not as appealing to have a triad but..." She blows out a breath and takes another drink. "I don't know. I'm not even sure what I'm asking you to do. All I know is that whatever is happening is dangerously precarious, and I'm worried about the fallout for Jasper."

I take a step around her.

"Thank you for telling me," I tell her, using that extra bit of Alpha nature even though it won't impact her as effectively as an Omega. She nods, the tension in her shoulders slowly leaking away. "I have no intention of putting Jasper in a situation where he has to choose between Rylan and me. I'll do my best to talk to Rylan about everything."

Not totally a lie.

Though there's probably going to be a fight before Rylan's willing to admit to *anything*. Good thing I don't have family dinner until Friday.

"Good. Let's go have some fun, then."

Just like that, a brilliant smile is lighting her face and she's walking back to the group. I blow out a breath and breathe out a low chuckle.

"All right, *piccolo fuoco*."

She raises an eyebrow. "Little fire?" She shrugs. "I've been called worse."

This time, my laugh shakes my chest.

Eighteen

RYLAN

I take the plastic takeout bag from the woman at the front of the restaurant, trying to offer a smile to mirror her own. Hers is more convincing. The cool air of the night forces me to take a breath but does nothing to soothe the raging mix of emotions roiling in my chest. I stretch my neck, trying to work through it without needing to punch something.

Or someone, really.

Of course he chose Dominic. I practically shoved him into the decision when I didn't stick around long enough to talk about what happened on Monday. I'd promised myself that if he asked, I'd talk about it. But the moment the question was halfway spoken, I ran to my room, hiding from whatever polite decline was perched on the edge of his tongue.

My phone vibrates, and I force a deep breath.

Last minute drop from Red Dog for a bonus track. You open tomorrow?

What time? Have a matinee.

Can you make 7 work?

Be there. Send the music so I can review it.

The last text is just a link that directs me to the guitar tab. I look it over, absolutely using it as the distraction it is.

For once, Mark's needs line up perfectly with my own. Recording isn't quite as good as working at the Haven for managing this festering *need*, but I can't risk not being able to show up for the matinee concert tomorrow. Ben will have my ass if I'm not there, and Owen doesn't deserve to put his neck on the line for me. Not after the fiasco that was my last scheduled shift at the Haven.

Between the music, the slight breeze, and the Chinese food that smells even better than I'd hoped, I manage to calm down enough to start the trek back to the apartment. I keep my mind blank, not allowing myself to think about the way Jasper looked at Dominic or the easy way they held each other around the orchestra. And I *certainly* don't let myself think about the way Jasper's eyes heated when he caught me staring across the bar, trying desperately to focus on whatever Simone had been saying.

Plastic cracks, and I force my hand to loosen on my phone.

"Goddamn it," I mutter as I inspect the cracks in the case. With a grunt, I shove the phone in my pocket before I can do anything worse to it.

The walk is just long enough—combined with the grueling marathon that is a Saturday evening concert—to tire me out enough that I don't entirely want to punch something when I round the corner of the block and see the apartment building. The darkness of the empty apartment both soothes me and feeds that festering rage. I set the food on the counter and grab my preferred practice guitar from its stand in the living room.

Twenty minutes later, I'm cursing whoever decided to key the new song in G flat *fucking* major and reviewing alternative chord structures. My breath catches as the front door opens. I force myself to not look up even as my fingers falter on the fretboard and one of my calluses catches, ripping open.

"Shit," I mutter, pressing the pad of my finger to my lips.

"Oh." Jasper's quiet shock has me forgetting myself and looking up from the floor. "Shit, sorry, Rylan. We can leave."

Dominic stands just behind Jasper, his shoulders filling out the door frame—something that if done by nearly anyone else would have heat rushing through me. Instead, a flash of jealousy races through me, and I have to swallow down a growl. His eyes lock with mine, and there's a cleverness there that has dread settling low in my stomach. It's the same look he had when we met at the café and he told me he wanted to form a fake pack.

Fuck, he plans to ask Jasper.

How can he be so casually cruel to *me*? He's cruel to others, sure, but he's never intentionally hung me out to dry like this. He has to realize just how much I'm agonizing over my temporary roommate. I shake my head, trying to tell him my thoughts on his plan without Jasper noticing, but it doesn't work.

Jasper—for once—notices what I'm doing.

"What's wrong?" he asks, taking a step away from Dominic. His brows furrow, but I'm caught up on how swollen his lips are. "Shit, you're bleeding. You want me to get something for it?"

Dominic grabs Jasper's hip before he can take a second step toward me. My gaze focuses on that point of contact. This time, I can't control the growl, the sound low and menacing even to my own ears. Dominic closes the gap between them, running his lips along the shell of Jasper's ear. He bites down on the spot just behind Jasper's ear, pulling the skin between his teeth until even I can tell it'll bruise again, and Jasper moans.

My growl gets louder.

Dominic smirks, and everything I'd managed to suppress since leaving the bar comes flying loose. Rational thought is gone, the need to mark Jasper as *mine* riding me harder than even the Omega's heat did last week. The memory of his body against mine, his mouth on my skin, more intoxicating even than her honeysuckle scent.

I'm across the room before I can think better of it and pushing Dominic away from Jasper. He doesn't fight me, dropping his arms away and pivoting so that Jasper stands behind him. He still has a smirk on his lips, that glint in his eye that tells me he's amused. It fans the flames of rage higher. I sink into it and let it take away whatever is left of my sanity. Before Jasper can say anything, I punch Dominic in the cheek.

Nineteen

"**D**ominic."

My voice is full of panic, and I silently curse myself. No one is going to calm down with me sounding like I'm a second away from hiding in fear.

I'm no stranger to a fight. Go to enough bar outings, and you're bound to see a couple. Seeing two Alphas go at each other? That's an entirely different experience.

The men circle each other, a light sheen of sweat coating Dominic's back as he blocks another punch from Rylan. His white shirt clings to the muscles of his back and the groove of his spine while his hair loses its pristine styling in favor of its natural black waves. Rylan snarls and launches at Dominic again.

"*Rylan.*" I manage to put a bit of bite into my voice as I realize there's more blood than there was when I first saw him on the couch.

I step up to them and try to pull the men apart, but it's like I'm not even there. Dominic, to his credit, seems intent on just dodging whatever Rylan throws at him, but he doesn't manage to miss all of them. Each heavy hit has me cursing under my breath. I shut the door and lock it before someone can hear the mess and call the police.

Dominic takes Rylan to the ground in a move so fluid, it's momentarily heartbreaking. It's clear he's the one used to dealing in violence. Rylan snarls and tries to force them to roll, but Dominic is too strong, even with Rylan's designation lending him more strength than I could ever dream to have regardless of how much of a gym rat I became. He forces Rylan's hands wide, and it throws Rylan off center.

I take the moment and dive between them, pushing Rylan off Dominic entirely. Forcing him onto his back, I straddle his thighs and cup his cheeks.

"*Rylan*," I say again with the same bite.

His lip is split, and a bruise already shadows his cheek and throat. It mirrors the snake tattoo on the other side, and the irony almost has me smirking. Almost.

Dominic doesn't move from where he's sprawled on the floor nearby. He's barely breathing, and I glance at him. His eyes are locked on Rylan, but his body is relaxed. His hands rest flat on the hardwood floor, and he doesn't seem concerned about his knuckles being split open.

"What the hell is going on?" I ask.

I don't move off of Rylan as he adjusts under me. I swing my gaze back to him just in time to watch his eyes flutter closed and his throat ripple with a heavy swallow.

"Sorry," Rylan mutters. "I can't... The idea of you being with anyone else sets me on edge. You being with *Dominic*? My best friend since we met at the Council's required classes? It's not something I can just sit back and take."

I drop my hands as shock courses through me. "What?" The question is barely more than a whisper.

Dominic grunts. "Be more honest than that, Rylan. I don't really feel like getting punched again."

"I want to fuck you," Rylan bites out, his eyes still closed. Lightning races down my spine and straight to my dick. He continues, his hands fisting at his sides. "Bend you over the closest surface until you're screaming for me. I could tolerate the need when we were just in the orchestra. But you here? In my space? The need is so strong that I can't... I can't fucking *look* at you without losing some of my sanity."

He sits up and looks at me. So close to him, I can smell the earthy scent of his arousal. "You showing up with *his* hickeys all over you nearly decimated my control. I fucking *need* you, Jasper."

I frown, confusion making me hesitate. He's describing how an Alpha reacts to an Omega. How could he possibly feel this way about me?

"But I'm a Beta," I say. His jaw clenches, and Dominic grunts, the sound low and derisive.

"So?" Rylan grips my throat, the same soft and controlling touch from Monday.

My blood heats.

I force myself to break his hold and stand, walking past them both and into the living room. Running my hands through my hair, I take a deep breath and try to understand what exactly happened.

"But you want to match. You want to register and be matched with an Omega and have a pack." As I say the words, the euphoria and desire induced by his touch fades. If I were Omega, I'd still be panting, needing his touch like I need air. My voice drops to a whisper, and the hopeless thread weaving through it is impossible to miss. "And I can't give you any of that."

"Maybe he doesn't need it," Dominic says. He sounds like

he's gotten up but hasn't gotten closer. I don't turn around to double check.

Rylan grunts. "Alphas need packs. Whether an Omega needs to be at the center is the argument."

Someone sighs.

"*Accidenti, amico.*" Dominic groans. "I am trying to help you. Stop being pedantic."

"Fuck off, Dom," Rylan mutters.

I run my hands over my face and turn back toward both men.

"What are you suggesting?" I ask without preamble.

Dominic leans against the island, his hands shoved in his pockets, his eyes locked on me. "Be with us both, *Tesoro.*"

My gaze snaps to Rylan. He's staring at Dominic, his eyes wide. His eyes close again for a heartbeat and then he glances at me.

"Dominic doesn't want children." I'm not entirely sure why I say it.

Rylan smiles, but it doesn't reach his eyes. "I'm well aware, Jasper."

"Somebody say something, then, because I don't know what the fuck is going on." This time, my voice bites.

Rylan glances at Dominic before crossing the room to me. "I want you. Dominic clearly wants you. I have no qualms with choosing to be childfree. Is this a dynamic you could be content with?"

The moment his hands graze my neck, something settles in me, a weightless feeling just under my sternum that I haven't felt since Seattle—since Violet. Rylan traces the chain of my necklace.

"Why an Omega symbol?" he asks, tracing the silver pendant.

"It was for someone I loved in Seattle."

Dominic speaks from across the room. "They were an Omega?"

I nod, my throat suddenly dry. "She is, yeah."

This will be the moment they realize I can't offer all of myself, that despite my best efforts, part of my heart still belongs to Violet and probably always will.

Rylan nods and tucks the necklace under my shirt without comment.

"So?" Dominic asks. "Is this something you want?"

Surprise has me hesitating. "You're not concerned that I'm still caught up over an ex?"

Rylan shrugs. "We all have baggage, Jasper. You're here with us now, not her."

Dominic crosses the room, standing behind me, his breath hot as sin against the sensitive spot just below my ear.

"Yeah, all right. Let's try it," I whisper.

The men don't hesitate.

Rylan grabs me by the throat, pulling me into him, grinding our hips together before slamming his lips into mine. He's rough and overbearing, and I melt at his feet because of it, each dominant touch making my dick ache and my heart race. He bites my lip hard enough that I gasp, and then his tongue is twisting into my mouth.

Dominic's low laugh against my throat is my only warning before he's bruising the sensitive spot just under my ear. He grabs my hips, pulling them back until I can feel the ridge of his cock against my ass. I groan into Rylan's kiss, and both Alphas chuckle.

"Fun fact," Dominic whispers into my ear. I shiver, melting against him, and he grinds against me. "Rylan and I have never shared before. He tends to like people that..." He bites that bruised skin again. My knees buckle, but he forces me to stay standing, his grip tight enough to bruise. "Well, they're not typically my type."

I pull away from Rylan.

"Bringing up past lovers when I'm caught between you two with the hard-on to end all hard-ons is not the best move, Dominic."

I mean for it to be dry, a little biting, but it's too breathless and desperate to hit that way.

Both men laugh. "Noted," Dominic whispers against my ear.

I shiver. Dominic traces the waistband of my slacks before undoing the button and fly. My breath catches in my throat, and I press forward into his touch.

"Which drawer?" Dominic asks.

My brain is already muddy, lust overtaking me as completely as the tide. I swallow and ask, "What?"

Rylan laughs, his grip tightening on my throat. The pinch has me pressing my hips harder into his. Dominic's hand gets caught between us, and I groan.

"Your lube, Jasper," Rylan says. "Unless you want me to get mine."

Twenty

JASPER

Lightning races down my spine at the soft caress of his words. I haven't been fucked in *ages*.

"Top drawer all the way to the left," I mutter.

The moment he moves from behind me, Rylan is undoing the buttons of my shirt and pushing it off my shoulders.

"I owe you," he says, dropping the shirt at our feet, ripping the bottom few buttons in his haste. "The next time you give me a blowjob like that and then walk out, I'm following you and forcing you to your knees. Understand?"

I groan. He drags his hands down my chest, letting his calluses and nails dig into my skin. His woodsy scent dominates the space, blending with Dominic's citrus like they were meant to be taken together.

A sentiment I wholeheartedly agree with.

"A man actually gave you a blowjob you liked?" Dominic tucks his hands into his slacks, his shirt nowhere to be seen. Had he taken it off while getting the lube?

The question dies in my throat as the sight of his body distracts me. His skin is a beautiful dark tan. Small scars overlay most of his torso, a larger, circular one just under the ribs. His hair is undone, the messy black waves falling on his forehead.

He's *gorgeous*. My dick twitches.

"Shocking, I know." Rylan's voice is dry.

Dominic hums and steps up beside him, his eyes intent on me. Somehow, I know the question perched on his lips, and I close the distance between us before he can ask it. His mouth is firm and warm, and I let myself sink into the feel of his kiss—more controlled and calculating than Rylan's—until my body glows with desire.

I pull away and sink to my knees, undoing his slacks and letting his cock fill my hands. Wordlessly, he hands off the lube to Rylan. Anticipation tightens my stomach.

Fuck, even his *dick* is pretty.

"Should be illegal how pretty you are," I mutter.

Dominic laughs. "My little sister hates it, too, if that makes you feel any better."

"I sure as fuck hope Alessia hasn't seen your dick, Dom," Rylan grunts.

I smile. Dominic starts to say something in Italian but cuts off as I take him in my mouth, letting my lips stretch around the head of his cock. He's large enough that my jaw aches after a few moments, but I ignore the discomfort, watching his face for what touches he prefers. He laces his fingers in my hair, cupping the back of my neck, as he starts murmuring in Italian.

Most phrases are too low and quick for me to understand, but when I take him deeper, relaxing my throat until the head of his cock touches the back of it, he bites out, *"Madre de Dio, Tesoro. Vai più piano."*

I pull away from him. "Quieter?"

He shakes his head and presses against the nape of my neck,

urging me back toward him. "Slower. I don't want to come before Rylan takes you."

Everything speeds up, all of us moving with a desperation that belies Dominic's easy words and Rylan's steady hands on my body. By the time I'm tasting Dominic's skin again, Rylan kneels behind me, spreading lube along my ass with the calm, confident touch of a man that's done it often.

I groan as he works into me, each finger a careful intrusion until I'm a panting, sweaty mess, trying to hold onto any thought as I take Dominic deeper into my mouth again.

"*Perfetto,*" Dominic murmurs. He cups my cheek, tracing over my lips stretched around him, and smiles. Their scents drown me, and I revel in it. An Alpha scenting for me is practically a miracle. Having two? It might just give me a complex.

I moan as Rylan pulls away, and the snap of the lube's lid rings through the space, overpowering Dominic's low panting. Rylan's invasion is slow and steady, and I'm trembling by the time he seats himself entirely, his hips flush with my ass.

"Fuck, Jasper," he mutters.

I moan around Dominic's dick, and both men laugh.

It takes an awkward couple minutes for us to figure out a rhythm that works. The moment it clicks, Rylan reaches around my hip and wraps his hand around my shaft, his hold tight enough that my stomach clenches. He strokes me, from root to tip and back, and I grab Dominic's thighs to keep from collapsing against him.

I'm going to be lucky to last minutes with the way he claims my body so completely.

It's like both men can tell it, too, because their movements speed up, Dominic's thorough claiming of my mouth forcing my mind to empty. Rylan moves behind me, his dick a slash of heat inside me that I didn't realize I craved so thoroughly.

"*Cazzo*," Dominic mutters. "Your mouth, *Tesoro*?"

I nod, looking up at him, holding his gaze as he falls apart. His lips are parted, his breaths sawing out of him, a thin sheen of sweat coating his body and making it even more appealing. He grunts, his pace faltering, and then I can taste him on my tongue, salty and earthy and *him*. I swallow as he pulls away, grinning at his low, choked groan.

Rylan grabs my throat and runs his teeth along the shell of my ear. I let my eyes flutter closed.

"Your turn," he whispers.

His touch disappears from me, and I cry out at its loss. His hand presses on the low of my back as he chuckles. I drop to my elbows, pressing my cheek to the cool floor, and try to catch my breath.

Holy *hell* can the man fuck.

His touch isn't gone for long, though, before he's stroking me again. That telltale feeling gathers at the base of my dick, and I groan. He picks up his pace, and whatever was left of my mind fades away, my body lost to the sensations he's forcing from it.

"Oh God," I gasp, fire shooting down my spine and through my dick. It twitches in Rylan's grasp. I feel the warm splashes of cum on my belly and sternum a moment before Rylan still behind me with a hard curse. He pulls out, cum lashing my back.

I sink to the ground and try to catch my breath. They don't allow me to for long. Dominic runs his hands through my hair and encourages me to roll over, running a soft washcloth up my chest. Rylan disappears into his bathroom for a minute before returning, his own dick hidden by a new pair of sweats.

Dominic tosses the washcloth toward the kitchen, and then pulls me into his arms, stretching out on the rug beside me. Rylan settles in behind me, and I allow my eyes to close again.

How the hell did I end up *here*?

Twenty-One

DOMINIC

Jasper shivers, goosebumps springing up across his back as I run my hand down his spine. He curls into me, pressing his forehead into my chest, his hand fisting against my sternum. The reaction has my purr kicking to life, and Rylan chuckles from where he lays on the other side of Jasper.

"Didn't know you could do that," Jasper mumbles against my skin.

Rylan laughs harder. "All Alphas purr. Even ones on small doses of rut suppressors."

Jasper grunts but plasters himself harder against me—an incredibly Omega move despite him being Beta. It's one of the things that attracted me to him in the first place, his inability to keep his hands off me at that pinball arcade bar.

"Not what I meant," he says.

I mess with the chain of his necklace.

"It's not instinctual with a Beta," I tell him. "Purring with one means there's more than just biology going on."

"And here I thought I just knew how to give a damn good blow job." He presses his smile into my chest, and I laugh, kissing his temple.

"Doesn't discount that you *do*," Rylan says, a wry lilt to his tone before he sighs and stretches. "Can we please move to a bed? This rug is not nearly as comfy as it looks."

I grab the shirt he ripped off Jasper and smack it across his chest.

"Fuck off, Dom," he mutters, rubbing his shoulders as he rolls to sitting.

Jasper sighs and pulls away, the moment effectively broken. His stomach growls, and Rylan springs into action before I can manage to lean against the couch.

"I brought Chinese food," he says, grabbing his abandoned shirt as he crosses the apartment, stretching his neck as he goes. "Didn't realize you would be here, or I would have gotten extra. I can order some more if you need it."

He cocks an eyebrow as he glances over his shoulder, and I smirk.

"I'll be fine, *amico*," I murmur.

I help Jasper to his feet, luxuriating in the fact he lets me dress him despite there being no biological urge for it. It's like he was wired specifically for me. No heats. No children. No ruts. Just naturally wanting enough touch and support to ease the Alpha instincts.

When I straighten, he cups the nape of my neck, pulling me into a languid kiss, his tongue exploring. I let him do as he pleases until my sated dick starts to twitch. His grip tightens, his nails scratching my skin, and I pull him closer, grinding my erection into his hip. The smell of grapefruit fills the room, overpowering the smells of sex and bodies from the earlier threesome.

Rylan groans. "Not yet. I'm too hungry for another round."

"You don't need to be involved," I mutter, palming Jasper's

cock over the top of his boxers. He grunts, pushing into me, and I smirk.

"*Dominic.*" Rylan's tone grows sharp, and I blow out a sigh, pulling my hand away from Jasper as I offer him a soft, chaste parting kiss. He intertwines our fingers, guiding me across the living space to the island's bar stools.

He offers me the plate Rylan sets in front of him, loaded with Szechuan chicken and fried rice. I ignore Rylan's frown, indulging Jasper in being able to care for me, remembering how much he smiled at the restaurant last week when I shared that dessert with him.

"I have an... unusual request," I say after a bit, once Rylan is settled on the other side of Jasper and focused on his own food. He glances at me, an eyebrow raised, but goes back to eating when I give him a single nod.

Jasper sets his fork down. "Like... you want me in a leather bodysuit kind of unusual? Or you want me to join you on a midday date to the pier that you loathe entirely type of unusual?"

He props his chin on his palm, a smile tugging at his lips, and I can't help but chuckle. Palming his thigh, I turn him toward me, bracketing his legs with my own as I invade what bit of personal space he has left. His breath hitches, and my purr starts again.

"Kind of surprised you didn't think about him coming up with a way to knot you," Rylan says, his nonchalance managing to add to the moment instead of detracting from it.

Jasper's eyes widen before flaring with heat. "Aren't those stimulants expensive?"

I shrug, but Rylan's the one that answers. "Yeah, but Dom doesn't care about cost. At least not until it hits five figures."

Truth.

Which brings me back to my problem.

"My request is more along the lines of registering with the

Council," I say, deciding to just get it out in the open and leave it up to Jasper if he wants to know why.

"I thought you didn't want to match," Jasper says, pulling away from me, his gaze wary. "No children. That's what we discussed at the restaurant. What I agreed to when I agreed to you both."

I nod, dropping my other hand to his knee, tracing the inside of his thigh. His pupils dilate as he takes a shaky breath, his dick pressing against his boxers.

"My trust fund matured this year," I say, squeezing his knee. "But my parents informed me last week that they won't release it until I've attended a damn gala. I have no intention of being matched."

Jasper frowns. "You can't guarantee that. Once you're at a gala, it's at the discretion of the Council."

"We could get matched with a male Omega," Rylan says softly. "And Dom could take rut suppressors when they go into heat if he really doesn't want to be involved."

Jasper twists, breaking my hold on him.

"One Alpha for an entire heat sounds awful," he says.

Rylan only shrugs. "Or we don't get matched at all. Most registered packs attend three before finally being selected for matching by the Council. Odds are we go, have a fun night of partying, then come back and build whatever we want together here. Dominic's parents release his trust fund, and we deactivate with the Council."

Jasper narrows his eyes. "You knew about this?"

Rylan blushes and ducks his head. Jasper twists back to me, suspicion in his gaze.

"He didn't know I wanted to ask you, just the ultimatum. I told him earlier this week after it happened."

That has him relaxing. He eats in silence for a few minutes, but I opt to watch him instead of digging into my own food.

After a few minutes, he pushes the plate away and stretches, lacing his hands above his head.

"No rigging it," he says, looking first at Rylan before back at me. "We do it properly. If there happens to be the exact perfect Omega for us there, we don't sabotage the match just to spite your family."

I cock an eyebrow, resting my elbows on the counter as I perch my chin on my fists. Absolutely not agreeing to that. Jasper and Rylan are enough for me.

It's an easy enough form to fill out, requesting the match be negated and the Omega matched with the second best option, but that doesn't mean it'll process before whomever is matched makes it out here.

Jasper reads my silence too quickly and far too accurately.

"That's the only way I say yes, Dominic," he whispers, dropping his arms to the counter, crossing them and tapping his forearm. "Those Omegas get one night and one chance. If, for whatever reason, the Council decides we're perfect for one of them, we give it our legitimate best. It's what they deserve."

Rylan catches my gaze from over Jasper's shoulder, nodding once, his lips pulled into a thin line. Wouldn't that just make him smug as hell? I go to all the work to make this a fake match up for the sake of the Council just to end up fucking paired with someone anyway. I shove the thought away.

The reality is that we probably won't even get shortlisted— the odds of being matched are even slimmer.

"All right," I agree, dropping my voice and enjoying the way Jasper shivers in response. "If for whatever reason we get matched, I won't sabotage it to spite my family."

He nods. I finally start eating.

"I suppose this solves my apartment problem," Jasper says, running his hand across his head, making his short hair stick up in little puffs.

Rylan glares, his lips bunching into a pout as he shoulders Jasper. "You know as well as I do that you weren't moving back into that little shoebox either way."

Jasper laughs, grabbing Rylan's chin and pulling him closer for a kiss.

His whispered voice is light and bright. "Just nice to hear you admit it, Rylan."

I focus on my food, giving them the small moment, organizing the to-do list that has now exploded for me over the next couple weeks. General profiles for each of us. Group picture. Proof of income. Proof of designation. Proof of address.

Cazzo.

Will they require me to stop the suppressor? The thought sours my stomach, and I set my fork down, running my hands down my face.

Jasper palms my thigh, pulling me from my thoughts.

"You sure about this?" he asks. I drop my hands and focus on him, his bright eyes seeing through me so thoroughly I wonder why I tried to hide my worry at all.

"*Sì, Tesoro,*" I murmur before kissing him.

"*Tesoro?*" Jasper asks against my lips. He doesn't get the accent quite right, but I smile anyway.

"Treasure," I murmur.

He hums and runs a hand down my chest. "I like the sound of it. You finished eating?"

I nod.

"Good."

Twenty-Two

SIX MONTHS LATER

RYLAN

I shrug off my backpack and guitar while kicking the door closed. I toe off my shoes and set the bag in the small front closet before walking into the open concept main floor of the estate. The living room is mostly put together, only a few straggling boxes littering the ground, their contents unpacked but not put away yet. Jasper must have spent today working on them all. The kitchen is similarly cleaned up, the only evidence of our move over the weekend the single box still unopened on the island counter. Next to it, a large envelope sits unobtrusively. The Council's insignia in the upper corner is the only marking anywhere on it.

I pick it up, trying to decide if I'm excited for it or not. Registering was always something I'd dreamed of—but knowing it's only temporary adds a different layer to everything. As does the fact that I've found contentment with Jasper and what we've created over the last six months.

As if my thoughts summoned him, his laugh echoes through

the house, bouncing off the still empty walls. I follow the sound, tucking the envelope under my arm as I move deeper into the place.

"*Tesoro*, you are messing with fire." Dominic's low baritone is nearly inaudible, but it's enough to know where to go.

It doesn't surprise me to find Jasper laid out on Dom's bed, his shirt missing and his sweats low on his hips. He murmurs a curse as Dominic leaves a hickey on his collar bone, one large hand keeping Jasper's arms locked above his head. Dominic's mouth trails down his sternum, and he arches on a gasp. There's not much more arousing than seeing Jasper submitting to Dom's particular flavor of control. A flash of heat shoots down my spine and settles in my groin.

I knock on the door frame, leaning against the threshold. Both men glance up just as I'm unbuttoning my dress shirt and letting it slip from my shoulders.

"You're back early," Jasper says. His eyes skate down my torso, and I smirk. The room is already overloaded with Dom's scent, but I don't hold mine back. It mixes well enough. Jasper groans.

"Is that the official notice?" Dominic pulls away from Jasper, releasing his hold and running his hand over his mouth. "It's early."

I shrug and hold it out. As Dominic gets up from the bed and picks up his own sweats where they had been forgotten on the floor in front of the bed, Jasper sighs and sits up.

"Six months, and you still manage to give me blue balls, Rylan," he mutters. His eyes are bright, though, and his shoulders relaxed, so I roll my eyes.

The moment Dominic grabs the envelope, I cross the room and push Jasper onto his back, running my tongue over his hip bone.

"I'll make it up to you," I murmur.

He shudders before cursing under his breath, and I chuckle. The moment my hands are on his cock, his moans are filling the room. I luxuriate in the sounds and scent and taste of him, letting the mixed feelings over being official drown under the satisfaction of having Jasper under me.

"Fuck, Ry," he grunts a moment before his cum is on my tongue.

I've barely swallowed and popped off of him when Dominic says, "Next gala is the end of the month. I'll get the travel details situated. Will you need paperwork for the philharmonic?"

"Fuck, Dom." Jasper laughs as he urges me toward his mouth. He presses a soft, languid kiss before rolling us so I'm below him. "Let it rest. We have time."

My chest is light, happiness making it warm. He smirks before he drops kisses down my throat. Dominic stays near the door, reading over something in the packet of information. I comb my fingers through Jasper's hair.

"*Dominic*," Jasper says, a bite to his tone this time. "We'll deal with it later. Come play."

Dominic sighs but sets the information on his bedside table. He strips out of his clothes without preamble, grabbing the bottle of specialty lube from the top drawer before settling behind Jasper.

He kisses the spot under Jasper's ear.

"All right, *Tesoro*," he murmurs. Jasper grins into my throat. I grind into his belly. "But only because you asked so nicely."

Acknowledgments

Every time I get to sit down and write one of these, I have the express desire to have someone pinch me. How can this possibly be my life?

Thank you, of course, to my husband, who has helped balance the raising of our children while being in school and working himself. You are always such a pillar of strength for our family.

Thank you to my girls! Our group chat is one of the best things that has happened over the last year, and I am so grateful for everyone's support and encouragement when I was struggling to finish this book. No friend group will ever quite compare to the special place you all have in my heart.

Thank you to Kiki and Rachel for continuing to take risks with me and helping me get better in this craft.

Thank you to Valkyrie for picking me up off the metaphorical floor when exhaustion and imposter syndrome were too much for me some days. Really, truly, you are a light in my life.

Thank you to Ande. You're my ride or die, but you know that already.

Thank you to everyone who loves and adores Omegaverse! You are such a bright and hopeful community, and I take great joy in knowing that I have a small place amongst you all.

About the Author

Jillian has been crafting stories since she was a young teen. She's always had a soft spot for heroines thrown into the deep end without any prior training. And while she, like most of Booktok, loves the dark-haired love interest, she secretly enjoys the blond Golden Retriever heroes. Other secret indulgences include the miscommunication trope, surprise or secret babies, and arranged marriages with age gaps.

Jillian enjoys soaking up the sun in Colorado. She can be found most days keeping the children and animals alive. During the summer, she enjoys testing the limits of her mental health by seeing how far into July she can remember to water the flowers and veggies in the garden. She spends most of the winter chasing after her snow loving children while silently cursing that she lives somewhere that actually gets cold.

instagram.com/jillianrink.author
tiktok.com/@jillianrink.author

Also by Jillian Rink

Serendipity Omegaverse

Ready or Knot

Knot Your Business

Amplifier Chronicles

Hidden

Haunted

www.ingramcontent.com/pod-product-compliance
Lightning Source LLC
Chambersburg PA
CBHW061545310726
48972CB00008B/2611